Max Elliot Anderson

Mountain Cabin Mystery

Max Elliot Anderson

Mountain Cabin Mystery

Winona Lake, Indiana

Mountain Cabin Mystery
By Max Elliot Anderson

Printed in the United States of America
Cover Art: Paul S. Trittin

Published by Tweener Press Division
Baker Trittin Press
P.O. Box 277
Winona Lake, Indiana 46590

To order additional copies please call (574) 269-6100
or email info@btconcepts.com
http://www.gospelstoryteller.com

Publishers Cataloging-Publication Data
Anderson, Max Elliot
        Mountain Cabin Mystery - Tweener Press Adventure
Series / Max Elliot Anderson - Winona Lake, Indiana
Baker Trittin Press, 2004

                p.   cm.

Library of Congress Control Number: 2004106295
ISBN: 0-9729256-3-5
        1. Juvenile   2. Fiction   3. Religious   4. Christian
        I. Title   II. Mountain Cabin Mystery
JUV033010

Dedicated to
the memory of
9/11

Chapter 1

Twelve-year-old Scott Holcomb slowly dragged his feet down the narrow sidewalk in front of his house toward a rusty mailbox perched on a weathered post. That same box had been responsible, over the years, for bringing his family both good news and bad. His father liked to say, "Sometimes I think we should just call it the bill box."

For three years in a row Scott had sent in his application, and in the first two years it had been denied.

If I don't get in this time I think I'll give up, he thought. He had been performing this same mailbox ritual every day for the past two weeks. Each time he had walked back empty-handed.

This year Scott had made sure he and his friends, Al and Benji, timed their applications to arrive on the very first day. That way he figured all three of their names would be at the top of the pile for consideration.

As he reached the mailbox, an uneasy feeling overtook his entire mind and body.

Scott bit down on his lower lip. "If it isn't here right now I'm going to scream," he said out loud.

Slowly, he opened the box. The lid came down at about the same speed as a river drawbridge. The sun's rays began to illuminate the inner darkness of the mailbox. Then reality struck. "It isn't there," he groaned. But when he looked closer, nothing else was in there. With a sigh of relief he said, "Good, at least the rest of the mail hasn't come yet either."

Scott lived in one of the older neighborhoods of Fox Valley. The cement walk up to his house had cracks where roots from towering oak trees forced some sections to move higher while others sank.

He walked back to the house being careful not to trip and went up the front steps and into the kitchen for lunch. Summer vacation had already begun, but the days were moving about as fast as a frozen trout stream in February.

"Mom, this is going to be the longest, slowest, saddest summer of my miserable life." Scott heaped chunky peanut butter on a slice of bread.

His mother was arranging spice bottles in a cabinet. With her neat appearance and sense of order, it was easy to see where Scott learned about having everything just right.

She turned to him. "You have a lot of fun things to do and friends to enjoy the time with this summer."

"Yeah, but they were counting on me to come through for them, and I just know it isn't going to happen."

"It's always important to have an alternate plan. You

shouldn't get your heart so set like this. It only leads to disappointment."

"What was that?" Scott shouted as he leaped from his chair and ran to the front window. "I think I hear the mail truck." Parting the curtains, he looked out only to see a blue van pass by with big yellow lettering on the side that read, "Big Joe the Plumber – We fix everything AND the kitchen sink."

"Sink rhymes with stink, and that's what this does," he muttered on his way back to the kitchen. He shoved the door open so hard it slammed against the inside wall.

"Now wait just a minute, young man!" his mother threatened. "You do something like that again and you're not going anyplace . . . even if you do get accepted."

Scott's father was a graphic artist and worked at home. He was in and out all day. He came in just then. "What was that noise I heard? Sounded like a sonic boom."

"Your son decided to start rearranging some of the walls in our house."

"Why is it whenever he does something wrong, he suddenly becomes *my* son?"

"Sorry, Dad, I'm just really frustrated. I don't think I can stand it one more day."

"It didn't come today?"

"No, but neither did the rest of the mail. I'm still hoping. I think I'll take my lunch and eat out on the front steps while I wait."

His mother smiled. "Good. At least you can't break anything out there."

"Okay, Mom."

He gathered his things and headed out to his post. *I feel like that old lady that lives across the street*, he thought. *She just stands there at her kitchen window and looks out all day long.* Scott figured his neighborhood would be safe as long as Mrs. Bollenbach was on guard.

After what seemed like forever, the mail truck finally came down his street. He hurried to the mailbox as the truck drove to the next house. With the speed of an automatic mail sorter, his eyes raced through the envelopes until he spotted one with a familiar logo.

"It's here!" he shouted. Then he ran back to the house, up the green painted steps, and into the kitchen. "It's here. It's here," he screamed.

"Calm down, would you?" his mother asked.

"And remember . . . it might be a rejection like the last two years," his father added.

"I know. I'm just so excited that's all." With trembling hands, Scott tore open the envelope. He slipped the letter out along with a colorful brochure. "This one has more stuff in it than the others did," he announced. For a brief moment, Scott fought off his fear of another crushing disappointment. His clammy hands were shaking so hard he almost couldn't unfold the letter. But as he lifted the top flap he saw the words, "Dear Scott,

Congratulations. This is to inform you . . . ."

That was all he needed to see. He dropped the letter, and as he streaked toward the telephone, he yelled, "I made it. I'm in. I get to go!" He grabbed the phone to call Al and Benji, his best friends in the whole world, but their mail hadn't come yet.

About five minutes after he hung up the phone, Al called back.

"Mine came, too. I get to go. Isn't that great?"

No sooner had Scott finished that conversation than the phone rang again.

"It's here. I'm so excited!"

"Great, Ben. Give Al a buzz and come on over. Bring your letters. We have a lot to talk about."

Scott, Al, and Benji went to the same school. Their birthdays were only three weeks apart. Al was thinner than Scott and had black shiny hair. His sharp, pointed features matched his equally sharp tongue at times. Benji was the smallest of the group. His curly blond hair and baby face made him seem younger than his friends. The boys soon arrived, and all three went down to the basement where Scott had set up a special room. Posters of mountains and climbers lined the walls. The boys put their acceptance letters on the table and then sat in beanbag chairs on the floor.

"Imagine," Scott sighed, "less than three weeks from today we'll be wilderness camping in the Colorado Rockies. Let's go over the things on the survival list and see what we still need to get before we go ."

Scott was the kind of person who wanted to have everything just right. He was a planner. His friends knew never to call and suggest for him to meet them and do something that hadn't been all laid out in advance. Although Al had often told him how annoying that part of his personality was, right now there couldn't be a better leader for their team.

"Now we can't fail our wilderness test," Benji sighed. "That'd be bad," Of course, he could find a way to worry about almost anything.

"We each need to get a down sleeping bag and a waterproof tarp," Scott continued. "My dad bought me this new hatchet. It's an Estwing. They're supposed to be the best. Look, it has a leather cover and everything so it fits right on my belt."

Al whistled, "Man, let me see that thing." Scott could see his friend was impressed, and Al was the kind of guy who didn't impress easily. "We could chop down a whole forest with this beauty."

"Remember what our wilderness teacher said?" Benji reminded them. "The trees are our friends. We should treat them like one of the family."

"I know," Scott groaned.

"I thought the animals and stuff are supposed to be for food and shelter. Isn't that the whole idea of the food chain?" Al asked.

"Yeah, and I'm sure glad we're at the top of that thing," Benji said.

Chapter 2

The next day, Scott stopped Al and Benji outside their wilderness class. "Remember, Al," Scott warned, "you can't do or say anything that might get us tossed out of here today."

"Don't worry. I won't."

"These people are real serious about some of the things they believe. You got that."

"Yup."

The boys quietly entered the room and sat together at the same table.

"Now class," the instructor began. "As you know, this is our last session before the test. We'll use it for review. Then our final period will be for the exam. Remember that if you fail the exam, you can't be certified for wilderness camping."

Scott glanced over and noticed Benji looked ghostly white. "You okay, Ben?" he whispered.

"Not really."

"Don't worry. We'll cram together."

"If you say so."

After the class was dismissed, the boys went outside to wait for their ride. Later that evening Scott found his father in his garage workshop in the middle of a woodworking project. His lathe spun at full speed as he turned a piece of wood. Chips from his chisel went flying everywhere. It was easy to see where Scott got his rugged good looks.

His father wore safety glasses and gloves. Because of his earplugs, he didn't hear Scott come up behind him. As soon as he'd finished removing just the right amount of wood from the piece, he stopped his machine.

"Dad, do you have time for a question about something? It's important."

"I always have time for you. Let's sit over on the bench away from this mess."

"Well, you know we've been taking all these wilderness classes."

"Yes. How's that going?"

"Oh, it's been great. I know how to make safe fires, what to do if a bear attacks, how to find nuts and berries, what snakes to look out for, and a bunch of other stuff like that."

"So what's the problem?"

"It bothers me . . . some of what our teacher has been telling us."

"Like what?"

"Well, remember when I was having trouble with evolution in my science class?"

"Sure do. You started wondering if you might actually be some monkey's uncle."

Scott ignored that remark. "Really, Dad. We've had it pounded into us pretty hard that Earth is a place we have to protect. Our teacher told us it would be better if we never went into the wilderness. She said people didn't have any more rights to air and water than the animals. Can that be right?"

"You're great at research. Why don't you do some searching on the Internet, and I'll see what I can find out from a couple of my friends and our pastor. How does that sound?"

"Sounds okay to me."

Scott did a little more checking on the Internet before he went to bed. During his search he came across a company developing water treatment plants that were different. He decided to email a few questions.

"My name is Scott Holcomb," he wrote. "I'm getting ready to go on a wilderness adventure hike with some friends. We're all twelve and go to the same church and school together. I was wondering if you have any information about how we should treat the environment. If you don't, that's okay. Thank you, Scott."

He ran a quick spell check and then hit send. *That's that*, he thought. *Probably never hear from those guys.*

He turned off his computer and got ready for bed. Next thing he knew the sun was shining in his face.

It can't be morning already, he thought as he rubbed the crispies out of his eyes. *Seems like I just went to bed.*

His mother called from downstairs. "Scott, telephone."

"Who is it?"

"Benji"

"I'll get it here . . . Hey, Ben. What's up?"

"I didn't want to say anything around Al, but I'm kinda scared about going on this trip."

"Really?"

"Yeah . . . I'm starting to think I might want to back out."

"How come?"

"Have you read the brochure from the camping place yet?"

"Huh uh. What'd I miss?"

"It sounds kinda terrible."

"Like what?"

"Oh, where should I start? Let me see. We have to watch out for bears. There are all kinds of plants that can make us sick. The weather could be yucky. It also has a bunch of pictures of the kinds of snakes we have to look out for. This could be bad, couldn't it?"

"I don't know, Ben. I think that's why we have grown-up guides to lead the group. These people have taken kids like us into the mountains hundreds of times. There's probably nothing up in those hills they haven't seen by now."

"Well, if someone had died on one of their trips, do you think they'd put a picture of it in the brochure and say, 'Here is one of the dead hikers we lost last year. So be careful you don't end up like him'? Somehow I don't think so."

"Of course not! But I did a lot of research on these people. They have a really good safety record."

"Says who? They could just hide all the stories of people who fell over the side or got eaten."

"I know it might seem like that, but do you remember how we had to get certified so we could go on the trip in the first place?"

"Yeah. So?"

"They have to do ten times as much as we did so they can be licensed to take us."

"I never thought about that."

"You mean you thought some people just got together, printed a nice brochure, and started walking off into the sunset leading a pack of campers to their deaths?"

"Well, no, now that you put it that way. Thanks, Scott."

"You're welcome. You and Al are still planning on coming over tonight, right?"

"I guess so."

"Oh, that sounds real definite."

"All right then. We'll be there."

"See you then."

"Bye."

Scott spent much of the day reading in the survival book his father had given him. He came to the part about the dangers on the trail. Benji was right. There was a lot to worry about. He was glad they wouldn't be lost out there alone with no one to guide them. That thought gave him a chill, especially when he came to the chapter about bears. *They look real dangerous*, he thought.

Scott invited his friends over for dinner, but on this evening his mother didn't have to cook anything. In fact, his parents went out for dinner because the hikers were going to try some of the trail foods he had bought online. Al took one look at the samples Scott had arranged in bowls on the kitchen table and groaned, "It's a good thing our guides are planning to make real food. I'd rather die than eat this stuff up there."

"The idea is to be prepared for anything. Suppose our group got stranded up in the mountains," Scott suggested. "I read about how a freak snowstorm can just blow up out of nowhere. We might be stuck for days with no way to get new supplies."

"That'd be bad," Benji muttered.

"Don't worry about it, Ben. They have it all figured out." He quickly changed the subject. "Okay," he continued, "we need to taste some of this stuff." For the next few minutes they sampled the trail mixes, dried fruits, beef jerky, and sunflower seeds.

Then Al had had enough, "You got any burgers? If I wanted to eat this kind of junk I'd just crawl around in my own back yard."

"Be serious, Al. It's all part of the planning."

"Well, then, I plan to stay real close to the camp cook."

"Whatever," Scott sighed, "but this stuff could be a life-saver."

"If it came to that, then I think I'd rather croak."

"Do we really need to be worried about running out of food?" Benji asked.

"See what you're doing here, Al? Now cut it out."

After they put the stuff away, they went back downstairs to work on their backpacks.

"We'll pack most of the extra food in Ben's bag since it's the lightest and he's the smallest. Any questions?" Scott asked.

"I got one," Al said.

"Okay."

"Does your Mom have any leftover fried chicken in the refrigerator?"

"Come on. Be serious."

"I *am* serious," Al complained.

"What if it gets freezing cold up there?" Benji asked.

"Oh, it'll be cold all right, but my dad taught me something about that once. You just stick your head inside your sleeping bag and breathe hard ten times."

"What does that do?" Benji asked.

"It works just like starting a fire. The heat from your breath warms up the inside of the bag. Then your body takes over, and you'll have all the heat you need. Here, let's open up your sleeping bag so you can try it." Benji untied the straps to his sleeping bag and rolled it out on the basement floor.

"I hope the ground won't be this hard."

"You worry too much," Al teased.

Benji proceeded to crawl into the bag. "It feels pretty cold in here right from your basement floor."

"Just zip it up with your head inside."

Benji did that. "Now what?" he asked in a muffled tone.

"Now breathe hard. Ten times."

"Why ten?"

"It doesn't matter, Ben. Do it eight times or twelve times. I don't care. Just breathe."

"Hey, it works. It's warm in here already."

"I told you."

"Cool," Benji said.

"Not cool," Al laughed. "Warm."

"Hey, somebody help me get out of this thing. My shirt got stuck in the zipper."

Al gave the zipper one hard pull, and it opened as smooth as a stone at the bottom of a mountain stream.

"Thanks, guys. I was really getting hot in there."

"So we're done here?" Al asked.

"I think so."

"Good. Then I'm going home and eating everything I can find in the house."

"You do that, Al."

When the boys left, Scott went back up to his room. He opened his email to see if he'd gotten anything new. Sure enough he spotted something from the wastewater company.

"Dear Scott,

"Thank you for writing. It's always nice to hear from young people who have the kinds of concerns you mentioned. It might interest you to know that several of us here are Christians. The ideas our company uses come right out of the Bible. If you are interested in more information about what we do, please let us know. We would be happy to answer any of your questions."

He printed out the message to make sure it wouldn't get lost. It was getting late, and Scott's parents weren't home yet so he decided to get ready for bed. Just as he had almost drifted off to sleep, he heard the garage door open. His parents didn't like to let the day end without at least saying good night. It wasn't long before they both came into his room.

"Are you still awake?" his mother whispered.

"Yes. Thank you for letting me go on this great trip. I can hardly wait."

"You're welcome, but we sure will miss you," his father said.

"And I don't care what you say," his mother added. "I'm going to worry about you from the time you leave until I see that smiling little freckled face come back from the mountains."

"Aw, Mom, there's nothing to worry about. We'll have grown-up guides that could do this kind of thing with their eyes shut. We should be totally safe."

"Well, I certainly hope so."

Chapter 3

The day of the big test arrived. "It should take about two hours, Mom. Hopefully we'll still be alive by then," Al joked, as the boys piled out of the van.

"Hey, it's a survival class," Scott reminded him. "The whole idea is for us to be alive at the end." They laughed on their way to the door. Scott thought that might have helped Benji just a little.

After their test, the boys headed out the door again to wait for their ride.

Al's mother drove into the circle drive, and they piled into her minivan. She could easily be Benji's mother because she worried a lot.

As they drove off, she asked, "Do you think you all passed?"

"I think if you wanted to drop us here we could live off the land starting right now," Scott boasted.

She began to slow the car and pulled slightly to the side.

"Not funny, Mom," Al complained.

"I was just kidding you guys."

"I think I still need to stay pretty close to my refrigerator, bathroom, and warm bed," Benji sighed.

Al looked over at Benji, "And probably all your teddy bears too!"

"Hey, the less I think about bears right now, the better."

"No kidding," Al added. "What did you answer for 'if you're staring a bear in the face'?"

"Alvin, you'd better do no such thing."

"Mom, p*lease* don't call me that."

"I don't care. You'd better not be planning to come within a hundred miles of any bears."

"But if we do," Scott answered, "we're supposed to be making a lot of noise in bear country. Then, if we really do see one, we aren't supposed to try to run away. And there's one more thing. Oh yeah, grizzlies are the meanest, and we should turn sideways."

"Right," Al added. "And whatever you do, do *not* look the bear in the eye."

"Hey, I got all those right," Benji yelled.

"Then, there are the parts about not traveling in the early morning or early evening, get behind a rock or tree, but don't try to climb them. There were a few more, but I forget," Scott concluded.

"Now, what about the mountain lions?" Scott asked.

When she heard that, Al's mother really did pull over to the side and stop. "Wait just a minute!" she shouted. "Exactly what are you getting yourselves into?"

"We're going to be with a bunch of people, for one, Mom. And our guides have experience with anything we could run into. I think that's why it costs so much."

"You're right about that," she said as she began to drive again.

Later that night the boys checked their scores on Scott's computer. All of them passed.

"So," Scott announced triumphantly, "that settles it. In only a few more days, the three of us are going to be out in the wild woolly woods. Look out bears. Here we come!"

It seemed as if they had waited a whole year since taking their final wilderness test, but finally they were cruising down the Interstate on their way toward Denver. Scott's father planned the trip so they could make it in one day. The way he had it figured, they should be pulling into the wilderness base camp just before dark.

A few hours later, Scott asked, "Hey, Dad, did you find out anything about that recycling stuff we were talking about?"

"Yes, I talked with our pastor. At first he looked at me kinda strange, like no one had ever asked him about that before."

"So what did he say?"

"Well, the main thing he told me is the environmentalists have sort of turned Earth, its rivers, and the air surrounding it . . . into a kind of god. Some people actually worship this place."

"Weird. I don't think I told you what that wastewater

company emailed me. The main guys there are Christians."

"Really?"

"The president of the company says that what they do comes right out of the Bible."

"Scott, you did a much better research job than I did, but I think it's like this. We have a house to live in. We all try to keep it clean, and we're careful not to damage it."

"Yeah, Mom would kill us."

"I'm not really sleeping," she teased. "Remember the kitchen door?"

"The way I see it," his father continued, "the world God created is like our house. In the same way, we should do our best to take care of it."

After one of the longest days the boys could ever remember, Scott's father called out, "Less than a hundred miles to Denver. Better start looking for the mountains."

"There's this kid at school," Al snickered, "who's a Bronco's fanatic. His dad took him to Denver once, and they went walking all around the city. They kept looking way up in the sky."

"What for?" Scott's father asked.

"They were looking for the Mile High Stadium."

"Man, that's one of the funniest things I ever heard."

"I don't get it," Benji complained.

"The city is a mile high above sea level. They thought the football stadium was up on top of something else that was another mile straight up. Man, how dumb."

"You boys will feel the difference when you start your hike. The air is thinner up here. If you have trouble catching your breath the first couple days, don't be surprised."

"I'm so excited, Dad. Hey, look, I can see the mountains!"

"Will it rain where we're going?" Benji asked.

"Oh, I wouldn't be at all surprised if it does. In fact, you might even be hiking right up into the clouds."

"Whew," Benji whistled.

After they got to Denver, Scott's father turned the car off the Interstate onto a two-lane road. It wasn't very long before they turned onto a road with barbed wire fences on both sides. As far as Scott could see, there was nothing in either direction.

A few miles farther Scott's father announced, "Look, there's a sign to your place."

The car turned off the two-lane road onto a narrow, dusty dirt road with two ruts for the tires and dried brown grass along the ridge in the middle."

"Are you sure we're going the right way, Dad?"

"For sure."

The dirt road began to climb almost straight up, making the going slow because of the heavy load of people and camping supplies. Scott's father flipped a switch, and the four-wheel-drive kicked in. The boys bounced all around in the back seat until the car reached the top of the hill where the ground flattened out.

Scott saw several other cars, pickup trucks, and SUV's

parked near a yellow and white striped tent with a big sign that said, "Welcome Wilderness Wanderers."

Chapter 4

"This is it," his father called. "Everybody out."

Immediately, two young men walked up to the car. Tanned skin on their legs, arms, and faces looked even darker against their sun-lightened hair. They wore uniforms of light green shirts and shorts. Scott noticed that their hiking boots looked like they'd been in a war with all the scuff marks and cuts in the leather.

"Welcome. We're glad you made it. My name is John, and this is Brian. We'll be your guides for the trip. There are thirty-five people altogether for this week."

"I'm Scott, and these are my best friends, Al and Benji."

"Glad to meet you, boys. There are a few others about your age. I think you're going to have a great time. Mom, Dad, it's time for you to leave so the adventure can begin."

Scott's mother didn't like the idea of leaving her little darling up there to face some angry mountain, and she started to let the entire world know it.

"Come on, Mom. I'll be fine."

"See that you are. That's all." Her eyes were glistening, but she did her best not to start crying in front of the whole camp.

"Well, boys. This is it," Scott's father said. "We'll meet you right back here in a week. Now, you take care and be very careful. Listen to your guides, and don't do anything stupid. A mountain is a beautiful *and* a dangerous place at the same time."

"We'll be careful, Dad. See you when we get back. And thanks again." As Scott's parents left for home, the boys turned, put on their backpacks, picked up the rest of their gear, and hurried into the tent.

Inside they found several tables set up. There were more people in the same color uniforms as their guides wore. Each had a clipboard. One person checked medical records. Another needed emergency contact information. Finally, they were assigned to a group which would be known as the Timber Wolves.

"This first night will be spent in base camp," John informed them. "We'll eat a great dinner, have a campfire, and get a good night's sleep. Brian plays a wicked blues harmonica, and if you ask real nice he might do a few tunes for you."

The boys were taken to meet the rest of the campers ranging from kids their age to people with white hair. Like them, this was the first wilderness camp for several of the people. Others said they had been up in the mountains more than twenty times.

It was almost dark when Scott and his friends had their campsite made up. The food was ready, and it looked delicious. They could choose from salmon steaks, bratwurst, pork chop sandwiches, salads, three kinds of bread, and one entire table that had been piled high with nothing but sweet things.

"I think I'll start there," Al said.

"Regular food first, then dessert," Brian told him. "Tomorrow you'll be glad you ate the good stuff."

Soon they were at their campsite getting ready for bed. There were nine people in the Timber Wolves.

"So, Brian, you going to play that thing for us or what?" Al demanded.

"Remember, you have to ask nice," John reminded him.

"Pleeeeeease," Benji begged.

The guide played two songs. Then he made sound effects like an old steam train, and played *The Orange Blossom Special*. The whole camp cheered when he finished.

"Hey," Scott asked, pointing at the stars, "What was that?"

"What was what?" Brian asked.

"I saw a big streak go all the way across the sky."

"Oh, you probably saw a shooting star."

"Really? How come we don't see those back home?"

"Because you spend most of your nights sleeping indoors with a roof over your heads."

"Well, yes."

"Out here, there aren't any city lights to mess up the night sky and we are higher in elevation, so the air is thinner. That's why the stars look brighter, and the sky looks blacker."

Al quickly pointed toward the sky. "There goes another one!"

"Better get to sleep now, guys. Big day tomorrow."

The campfires began to dwindle, making the night darker still. Scott was glad to have his two best friends nearby. This was a big trip they were taking, and he wanted to enjoy every minute. At the same time, he had an uneasy feeling inside. He wasn't sure they could keep up with the more experienced hikers, and he hoped no one got hurt.

After what seemed like only a little catnap, Scott opened one eye. It was still dark out, but he could see a few people moving around in the camp.

What are these people doing up in the middle of the night? he wondered. He reached over and pushed the button to light up his watch. It was 6:00 A.M.

"Morning already?" he groaned. The cooking stoves were burning, and there was the sweet smell of bacon and eggs frying. He was pretty sure he could smell maple syrup.

Ummm, he thought. He slid out of his sleeping bag and woke up his friends.

"This is the day we've been waiting for, for three years. Come on. You don't want to sleep through it."

Benji stretched and yawned, "I don't?"

"No, you do not."

"Okay. You've convinced me, I think." Together they shook Al until he was somewhere between dreamland and real life.

"What, what's wrong?" he asked groggily.

"It's only morning, you slug," Benji teased. "Time to wake

up and smell the . . . yum, whatever you want it to be. It all smells so good." Soon they were sitting on long log benches eating like truck drivers.

"Will we have food like this on the trail?" Scott wanted to know.

"We get food delivered to each campsite," John told them, "but I have to warn you. As good as the trail food is, this is some of the best you're going to get so I'd advise you to eat up."

"Think I'll stuff my pockets," Al suggested.

"Fine with me if you want to. But you might as well stick a big sign on your back that says, 'Calling all bears.'"

"Oh . . . right. I remember. You aren't supposed to get food smells on you."

"Exactly. If a bear smells bacon and eggs on your poncho, he might invite *you* over . . . for breakfast."

Benji shuddered, "I'd rather not."

The guide in charge of the whole camp stepped up to the front where the campers were finishing breakfast. His rugged features made him look like a man who had made this trip a thousand times.

"Listen up," he growled. "Throw all your trash in the bins, go get your gear, and meet me back here in ten minutes. We have a full day's hike to our first campsite, and I *know* you don't want to get there in the dark."

"Come on you guys; let's hurry," Benji begged his friends.

Soon, they were on the trail leading up toward the high

mountains. Scott liked the scent from the evergreens that grew wild at this elevation. They walked on a dirt trail that was quite narrow. Occasionally someone slipped and fell down.

"Road kill!" a guide would call out. The first trail also cut through a ranch where several cattle grazed.

"Hot stuff!" another guide warned. That meant to watch where you were walking for the next few steps. It wasn't long until the trail began to angle upward. It narrowed even more while the dirt gave way to more and more rocks. The going became extremely difficult causing Scott and his friends to choose their steps with great care.

Scott realized that his father had been right. He found it harder to catch his breath. He was glad he and his friends had taken the class, too. Of course, they couldn't even be on the trip if they hadn't. But he liked putting into real life the things they had only heard about before.

"It's a good thing we wore hiking boots," Benji said.

"I would have blown a tennis shoe by now," Al joked.

Farther and farther they went, looking like a human mule train. Someone started mooing like a cow, another person made sheep sounds, and the whole group started laughing.

They made their way around a bend in the trail that took them between sheer rocks on all sides. At that point there was nothing to do except follow the person right in front, like elephants in a circus. The farther they walked, the narrower the trail became until it opened into a wide flat area made of solid rock.

The leader called out, "Lunch! Sit down, and take a load off. We'll eat in about thirty minutes."

"What are we having?" Benji asked.

"We don't want to take the time to cook on the trail," John told him. "We save that for supper and breakfast in each campsite. We're having subs and finger food at this stop."

Soon, people were sprawled out all over the place eating their sandwiches like it was the first food they had seen in a week.

Scott turned to John, "How many times have you been on this trip before?"

"Let's see. This is my sixth . . . no, seventh time. And Brian there, shhh, he's sleeping right now. This is his fourth."

"Fifth, John. It's my fifth."

"Hey, he talks in his sleep."

"Has anyone ever gotten hurt up here?"

"You bet they have."

"Honest?"

"I'd like to say it never happens, except it does. But almost every single time, it's usually been because someone did something stupid or they weren't paying attention. That's why we make sure you get certified. At least then you know what to expect and how to be prepared."

"Well, what have you seen happen?"

"Oh, broken legs, head injuries, things like that."

"Then what?"

"It's usually a guaranteed ride in a helicopter down to the medical unit."

"That sounds like fun," Al thought right out loud. "I'd love to ride in one of those things."

"Not if your head's split wide open, you wouldn't."

"That'd be bad, wouldn't it?" Benji asked nervously.

"Yes, it would."

Chapter 5

After they finished eating, Scott, Benji, and Al stretched out on the rocks. Benji grunted and groaned. "How come food tastes better out here than at my house?"

"Don't ever let your mother hear you say that," Brian warned.

"Food always tastes better out on the trail. No one knows why for sure," John added. "Tonight we'll have a huge cookout."

"Like last night?" Al asked.

"Better."

Soon, the snake-like line of hikers wound its way along the trail once again. This part of the hike went a little easier because the trail was wider as it crossed over flat rock. Their trail took them through the higher valleys of the foothills prior to turning upward into the high mountains.

"This is easy," Al commented.

"Enjoy it while it lasts," John told him.

"While it lasts?

"By this time tomorrow you'll be much higher, and the

going gets really rugged."

"I can't wait," Benji moaned.

From this level the boys could see over the tops of some of the trees. At one point the hikers had to pick their way across a mountain stream over large boulders. It almost looked as if someone had built the crossing that way.

"Did you guys make this so we could get across?" Scott asked.

"No. Someone much bigger than any of us did that a long time ago," Brian answered. After a few more hours of walking and several rest breaks, the group came into a large clearing. It was surrounded by trees so tall they seemed to touch the clouds.

"We camp here for the night," the leader announced. "Set up your own area. We'll start a big campfire in the center ring. Supper will be in about an hour."

Everyone scattered into smaller groups to get things ready for the night. It wasn't long before it looked as if they had been set up there for days. The cook rang his dinner bell. That's all the boys needed to hear, and they leaped to their feet. Tired as their legs felt, they scurried over to the serving line.

"Hot dogs, burgers, anything you want, and as much of it as you want," the cook said proudly. The boys ate, and ate, and ate.

"I'm going to gain a hundred pounds on this trip," Al complained.

"Not really," Brian corrected. "You eat it at night, and you will walk it off the next day."

"No kidding!"

After supper the cook brought out several large bags of marshmallows, graham crackers, and milk chocolate bars. "You can toast marshmallows on these sticks, or you can make smores. It's up to you."

"And you thought you were full, Benji," Al teased. When everything had been cleared away, the guides gathered around the big fire. Scott noticed a couple of guitars.

"Tonight we're going to sing some old camp songs," the leader announced. "I hope you didn't leave your good voices back down at base camp."

"*Base* camp. That's pretty funny," John laughed. "Brian here can sing tenor."

"Is that right?"

"Yeah, I sound pretty good *ten or* twelve miles away."

The whole camp proceeded to sing songs including *Oh My Darlin', She'll be Comin' Round the Mountain, Row, Row, Row Your Boat,* and a few the boys had never heard before.

"Does anyone know a good outdoors joke?" the leader asked.

"I got one about an animal," a voice called out from the darkness. "I'm a veterinarian, so it's a veterinarian joke . . . well, sort of."

"So tell it already," another voice prodded.

"Okay, here goes. This veterinarian put himself through school working nights as a taxidermist. For you younger kids here tonight, that's a guy who stuffs animals after they're dead. Anyway, when he graduated from veterinary school, he decided to combine the two jobs."

"How did that work?" a camper asked.

"He figured he would take care of all his customer's needs, and at the same time double his income. When he opened his office, he had a big sign painted. It said, 'Hillcrest Veterinary Clinic and Taxidermy – Either way, you get your cat back.'"

A collective moan swept through the camp.

"Either way, you get your cat back," he repeated.

"We got it, trust me, we got it," another camper groaned.

"I found a pretty funny one on the Internet about fishing," Al ventured.

"Okay, we'll bite," someone laughed.

"Well, this guy went ice fishing. He took out his big drill to cut out a fishing hole. Then a very loud voice from above boomed, 'There's no fish there!'

"So, he tried in a second spot. Again the loud voice told him, 'There's no fish there either!'

"He decided to try a third place, and once again the booming voice said, 'None there either!'

"Now the fisherman started getting a little nervous. So he asked in a shaky voice, 'Are you God?'

"After a long pause, the voice answered, 'Nope. I'm just the ice arena manager.'"

That sent a roar of laughter through the camp. "You're going to hav e to be our official camp humorist," the leader declared. "Tomorrow we start walking almost straight up. I would advise you to get an extra good night's rest. You're going to need it, trust me."

The boys were soon snugly inside the safety and comfort of their sleeping bags.

"I just breathed ten times in here," Benji reported in a muffled voice. "Now, I could bake potatoes in this thing."

"Just sleep in it, will ya?" Al said.

In no time, the sounds of sleep drifted across the camp. It had been a hard walk with their heavy packs in the thinner air. Scott lay on his back and looked at the wonder above him. The canopy of stars shined so clear and bright, he felt as if he could reach out and take them in his hand. It reminded him of the time his parents took him to the planetarium for a show about constellations, but that was nothing like the show he had now.

Right then he began to remember the conversation with his father and the emails he had gotten about taking care of Earth. He didn't want to do anything to destroy the beauty he had already seen in just one day on the trail.

His father had told him, "God created all things for our use. He expects us to take good care of the gifts He's given us. If you keep that in mind, then you'll have it right."

Scott was pleased that for as long as he could remember, the family never took a road trip without a litterbag in the car for their trash. At the same time, he saw other people throw things out their windows as they streaked along the Interstate.

Wonder why people do that? He thought as he finally drifted off to sleep.

When he awakened the next morning, it felt as if the sun hadn't come up yet, but it wasn't exactly dark anymore either. As his eyes slowly adjusted, he noticed that a thick heavy fog covered the surrounding area like a cold gray blanket. The outside of his sleeping bag was all wet, too, but it wasn't raining.

"Burrr," he shuddered, "it's cold out." He sniffed the air and detected the definite evidence of bacon, sausage, and eggs. Over by the camp stove, Scott saw the cook had already been hard at work. The breakfast bell hadn't rung yet, but he woke up Al and Benji so they'd be ready.

"What's the big hurry?" Al complained.

"It's okay with me. Don't eat if you're not hungry."

"Not hungry? Who said I wasn't hungry?" Just then the bell did ring.

"Breakfast!"

Quickly the boys found their way to the serving table and took their place in line. Brian was just in front of them.

"Can me and my friends sit with you?" Scott asked.

"Sure thing."

Scott proceeded to stack a little of everything on his plate. In addition to the things he'd smelled cooking earlier, he also saw French toast, blueberry pancakes, biscuits, fruits, juices, milk, and cereal.

"You sure know how to make good food," he told the cook.

"Well, thank you for the compliment. I do my best."

"You *sure* do," Benji added.

The boys walked over to some large rocks in another area of the campsite and began to devour their breakfast.

"So Brian," Scott asked, "is this what you do all the time? For a living I mean."

"Can't."

"Why not?"

"Because long about November, you'd be up to your armpits in snow if you were still standing in this place."

"Really?" Benji asked.

"Or deeper. But since you asked, when I'm not up here taking groups into the mountains, I'm a youth pastor in a church down in Denver."

"No kidding? Us three guys are in the same Sunday school class back home."

"That's wonderful."

"So how does your church let you come out here for such a long time?"

"You should ask how my wife lets me. There really are a couple of good reasons. Eventually I'll probably lead our church youth group on a trail hike once a year. So they consider this good training. The way I look at it, I get to meet all kinds of different people out here. That way I think I'm more prepared for my work, and the church gets a better youth pastor."

"Cool," Al commented.

"Then could I ask you something?" Scott said.

"Sure."

"Before I came out here, my dad and I started talking about environmentalists and Christians."

"Oh, boy, don't get me started on that one."

"Why not?"

"Because this is where the camping trip would end. We wouldn't finish talking till the snow falls."

"Well, I know there's a lot to it, but what do you think?"

"It's interesting you'd ask because the paper I'm writing for my Masters Degree is on this very subject. See, when I started leading camping groups, I had it all wrong."

"How?"

"I thought Christians couldn't run far enough or fast enough to get away from the subject."

"Well, what changed your mind?"

"It was the people I met, Scott. They really broke my heart. They were coming up on these hikes not just to be close to nature. Some of them actually worship the environment."

"You mean like rocks and trees and stuff?"

"Not exactly to that extent, but pretty close I'd say. To put it another way, I've come to see that some people have it all twisted. They wind up worshiping the creation but totally miss out on the Creator."

"Humm."

"Tell you what. When I finish my paper, I'd be happy to email you a copy. You might be able to use some of the information for a report or something."

"Wow! Would you?"

"Sure thing."

"All right everyone," the director called out. "Time to rack it up, pack it up, and stack it up. Those mountains aren't going anywhere, but we'd better. But before we do that, there are two rules for today. We're going to enter bear country this morning. With this fog, that could be a bit tricky."

"Great," Benji whispered.

"So if I see anything, I'll give you the signal. Be sure to make a lot of noise. You can sing if you want to, clap your hands . . . anything like that. And if you see any special gifts that a bear might have left for us in the trail, make sure to call out, 'Hot stuff,' so the person behind you doesn't ruin a perfectly good pair of hiking boots." That made everyone laugh.

"Well, what are you waiting for," he barked. "Let's get to it. We need to hop on down the bunny trail."

The campsite burst with activity as people rolled up sleeping bags, zipped their backpacks, and prepared to move out. Scott looked forward to the next few days on the trail. It felt to him like he had just discovered a new big brother in Brian.

A few minutes later the line of campers was under way. Scott, Al, and Benji found themselves at the very end of the line, but that was okay because Brian was with them. The trail they were taking this morning quickly narrowed.

Heavy dew from the night before made the rocks especially

slippery. Thick fog still hung in the area, but they managed to make good progress. Then Scott looked up the trail to see that part of the line of campers had already disappeared into the cloud cover.

"Will you guys be all right for a couple of minutes?" Brian asked. "I need to run up ahead for a second." Scott nodded, and Brian sprinted toward the front of the hikers.

The trail made a sharp turn to the right so it was important to pay attention to every step. Suddenly Benji gasped, "Hey, you guys. Look!" He pointed over into some trees and thick brush.

"I think I see a deer. Quick! Al, get your camera." Al and Benji darted off the trail in the direction where Benji had pointed.

"You guys," Scott protested, "get back here right now. We aren't supposed to leave the trail. Ever!"

The other two paid no attention to him. Al pulled out his camera while he and Benji slowly inched forward and then crouched into position behind a boulder. Al took careful aim, and when the flash went off, it lit up the fog in all directions.

"Hey, my flash made everything disappear."

"Yeah, well it had the same effect on the deer. You guys need to get back up here." His friends searched a little longer for the deer then scrambled back up onto the trail. As they began walking toward the other hikers, they couldn't see anyone. "Now you've done it," Scott grumbled. "Hold on a minute, let's stop and listen. Maybe we can hear something." They craned their necks but still heard nothing.

Scott began leading them forward. "We'd better start running so we can catch up. Sooner or later they'll see we aren't with them and send someone back to get us."

On the steep, wet trail, the boys couldn't make very good progress. Their heavy packs didn't help much, and that thin mountain air was a killer.

"I need to rest," Al grunted. He sat right down in the middle of the trail.

"We can't take the time. Now get up."

Al struggled back to his feet, then slumped right back down. They rested for a couple more minutes and then started off again. Soon, the boys came up over a rise, but they were completely surrounded by the fog. Then Scott saw something that made his heart almost stop beating. There, directly in front of them was a sign. At this point, all hikers had two choices; they could go left and higher up the mountain or right and lower toward a ravine.

"Which trail should we take?" Al asked nervously.

"I don't know. We've been hiking *up* for a long time. I don't think they would keep doing that for the whole day."

"So what do you think?"

"I say down."

"Are you sure?"

"No!"

"Well, if we make the wrong choice, we'll be lost forever."

"I know it."

"Shhh," Al cautioned. "I think I hear something . Down . . .

definitely down."

They sprinted down the trail to the right until Scott brought them to an abrupt halt.

"Okay, *now* let's start yelling."

Benji looked at Al, then over to Scott,

"This could be bad, couldn't it?"

Chapter 6

After a few good screams without hearing any answers, the three lost hikers continued hurrying in the direction they were certain the others had gone. At first, the descending trail made their going a little easier, but soon it changed until they were into the most difficult climb of the hike so far.

"This can't be right," Al complained. "Some of those older people could *never* make it up here." A little farther along, the trail turned into a narrow shelf with sheer rock on one side and what looked to be an endless drop-off on the other.

They continued inching their way upward until Scott groaned, "That's it. We're turning back. We already broke the first rule when you get lost. Remember?"

"Yeah, and I got that one right on the test," Benji complained.

"Well, I didn't," Al said. "What were you supposed to do next?"

"You're *supposed* to stay put, right where you are. At least then you have a better chance of being found."

"We can't be that far off track. Let's just go back where we came from," Al suggested.

"What was that?" Benji asked in a half whisper. "I heard a growl."

"It's probably my stomach," Al joked. "I'm already getting hungry again."

"Be quiet," Scott whispered. "I heard it, too. It's coming from behind us."

Suddenly, a big, ferocious-looking bear emerged from the fog. He was walking up the narrow trail and coming right toward them. The menacing dark brown bear stopped in the middle of the trail and stood up on his hind legs. Even though he wasn't close yet, the boys could see that this bear was a lot bigger than any one of them.

As he sniffed the cold mountain air, blasts of white steam bellowed out of the bear's nostrils. He seemed to look in the direction where the boys stood. As he did that, he opened his jaws to reveal long, sharp, yellow teeth. It's what he did next that made the already frightened boys wish they'd never come up that mountain.

The bear began to growl as if he hadn't had his bear breakfast yet. Then, he dropped back down on all fours and began lumbering up the trail again.

"I didn't think something that big could get up that narrow trail!" Scott exclaimed.

"Try telling that to the bear," Al muttered through clenched teeth. Benji pulled biscuits out of his pockets and threw them down the trail toward the bear.

"You aren't supposed to have food on you either."

"I forgot about that." he confessed.

"This is just great. You guys stop to take a stupid picture, and now look at us. We need to move it. Those things are faster on four legs than we are on two."

"Especially with our packs," Benji complained.

"Whatever you do, don't run, and do *not* look that bear in the eye."

"Who's looking?" Al said.

"All right then, let's start walking, nice and easy."

They began to ease their way on up the trail. As they moved, the bear kept right on coming. That big, four-legged eating machine walked right past the biscuits Benji had tossed. He continued climbing directly toward the boys. Quickly, Scott looked around for an escape route. Then, he saw it. "Guys," he whispered, not even moving his lips. "See that narrow place over my right shoulder where those two big rocks come together?"

"Yes," they whispered back.

"It looks big enough for us to squeeze through but too narrow for fatso back there. I know you aren't supposed to run, but it's so close. I think we can make it before he gets to us. Are you guys up for trying?"

"Uh huh," they whispered with their eyes stuck wide open.

"We've only got one shot at it. When I yell, you'd better be right behind me because I won't be looking back."

The bear was only about twenty-five feet away now. In seconds he would be right on top of them.

"LET'S MOVE IT!" Scott screamed. In one fluid motion the boys were pushing their way between the rocks.

"I hope you're right about that monster being too big," Al cried. Scott was the first one through. Even with his backpack he still made it. Al was next with Benji bringing up the rear. Just before he came to the opening, Benji slipped on a wet rock and hit his knee, really hard.

"Ow," he howled as he stopped for just one second. That gave the bear the time it needed to catch up.

"Ben, don't look back! Just run! Fast!"

"Hurry, Ben, hurry!" Al warned. Benji did what they told him, and immediately he was pushing his way through the narrow opening. "Help me! I think I'm stuck."

"Get out of your backpack," Scott ordered.

"I'm trying. I'm trying!" Benji kicked his feet wildly, desperately trying to break free.

Al grabbed one strap while Scott gripped the other. Together they yanked them from Benji's shoulders just as the bear reached through the opening and swiped with one giant paw. His long sharp claws instantly cut the back of the pack to shreds. Al and Scott took Benji by the shoulders and yanked him through the opening. They all landed in a heap.

Benji turned back just in time to watch with the others as the bear stuck his head through the gap in the rock, opened its mouth, and showed its full set of sharp, yellow teeth. He roared so loudly that it seemed to make the ground shake. At the same time, he used his powerful claws to pull the contents of Benji's pack to the other side of the opening.

"My mom is *really* going to be mad. That backpack cost a lot of money."

"It could have been you on the other side of the rocks with that bear," Scott reminded him.

"Now, what are we going to do? All our extra food was in that pack . . . even some you guys didn't know about."

"You'd be bear breath right now if we hadn't pulled you loose," Al said.

"I hate to say I warned you, but don't you guys remember talking about the kind of food we were supposed to bring? It was just for an emergency like this. And you, Benji, why didn't you just paint a target on your backpack. You were practically a walking fast food restaurant out here. I can't believe you did that."

"I know. I'm sorry."

"Sorry doesn't cut it right now. We are in serious trouble, guys."

"One thing's good," Al noted. "At least the bear can't come through there and get us."

"Yes, but we can't go back that way either. Now can we?"

"Oh."

"Empty out your pack. Let's see what food and water we

have between us."

Al and Scott dumped everything from their backpacks onto the ground. "From what I see, we have enough trail mix to cover breakfast, lunch, and dinner three times over," Al groaned.

"I'm not even going to tell you guys what was in my bag."

The boys could hear the bear destroying the contents of Benji's backpack on the other side of the narrow rock passageway.

"Well, we have plenty of water. That's something we really have to be careful about so we don't get all dried out. At least if we find more up here, it'll be coming from melted snow."

"So it should be clean?" Benji asked.

"Sort of. But we're going to have to keep going. Right now, nobody knows where we are."

"The bear does."

"Al, do you ever stop? Let's just go."

"Hey, Benji, was that a black bear or a grizzly?"

"Who cares?" Benji answered.

"Well, you were the closest one to him."

"Don't remind me."

Scott noticed right away that this trail wasn't like the one they had been on before. It didn't show the same amount of wear. There were no footprints. Grass, weeds, and a few wildflowers grew in all the spaces between the rocks. "Looks like nobody has walked on this trail for a long, long time."

"I think you're right," Benji agreed.

They continued walking for the next couple of hours. Since Benji didn't have his heavy load any longer, he quickly moved to the front of the line. The hikers, Huff and Puff, struggled trying to keep up with him.

"Hey, Ben, slow up. We need to stop and catch our breath." The boys sat beside the trail for a few minutes.

"It feels so good to get this thing off my back," Al groaned as he let his pack hit the ground.

"Let's go ahead and eat something while we're here," Scott suggested.

"Humm," Al said. "Let me see. What shall I eat? Trail mix? Trail mix? Or . . . trail mix? I know. I think I'll have some trail mix thanks to my good friend Benjamin."

"Come on you guys. I'm *really* sorry."

"Why in the world do you think we bothered to take all those classes and the test that almost killed you? It was for something exactly like where we are right now."

"I know."

"Lay off him, Scott. He feels bad enough already."

"That's not the point. Not the point at all. We might not get out of this place. Have you thought about that?"

"Yeah, I have. It reminds me of that story from church about the shepherd and his sheep. Do you remember it?"

"You're the story teller. How about you telling it to us."

"Well, this guy had a hundred sheep, but when he brought them home for the night and counted them, he noticed one was missing. He could have said, 'Oh, well, I have ninety-nine others. What's the big deal about one little lost sheep? I can get more.'"

"I remember that story," Benji spoke up. "He left all the rest and went out to find the lost sheep. That was one of my favorite pictures . . . the one where the shepherd came back carrying the lost lamb on his shoulders. My mom had it laminated for me. I use it for a bookmark." He took a deep breath and sighed, "I miss my mom."

Just then, a small sparrow landed on a branch above Scott's head. It was so close he could almost reach up and pet it. The little bird sang out like a choir of angels at that moment. The boys listened to him until he had finished. Then, as quickly as the little bird arrived, he flew away again.

"You guys are right. I'm sorry. It's just that I feel sort of responsible for all of us. One thing's for sure: God knows where we are even if no one else does. He's watching us right now, and He'll take care of us. You wait and see."

That made everyone feel a lot better. They finished their rest break, put away the trail mix, and stood up to leave.

"Anyone want some dried apricots for dessert?" Benji asked.

Scott looked at him with surprise, "Where did you hide those?"

"I don't even want to know," Al said.

Each boy enjoyed the treat before they hiked deeper into uncertain territory. Thoughts of the bear, even though they'd survived a serious attack, began to fade from their thinking and conversation.

"I'm feeling pretty good now," Scott announced confidently. "I think the worst is behind us. All we need to do is follow this trail. It has to come out someplace. Hey, Al, you still have that ball of string you were supposed to carry?"

"Got it right here." He pulled out a roll of white kite string.

"We should mark our path. That way people might see which way we went. We can make arrows out of sticks on the ground to show the direction we walked."

"That's a great idea," Benji said as he took a knife out of his pocket. "I'll be in charge of string cutting."

"And I'll tie them on bushes every hundred feet," Al said.

"While you guys do that, I'll take care of the direction arrows."

Having jobs to do helped take their minds off the trouble they were in, and it made the time go faster. That really wasn't such a good thing, though, because it meant, sooner or later, it would be getting dark.

On and on they trudged not knowing what lay just around the next twist or turn. Then, Al stopped, "Wait a minute. I think I hear something."

"That isn't funny Al," Scott warned.

"No, I mean it. Listen!"

"Tell me it isn't another bear, you guys. I don't have a backpack to give him."

"Sounds like water to me," Scott said. "I think it's just over that ridge."

They moved quickly toward the sound. They thought it would be right around the next boulder or fallen tree, but they saw nothing there.

"The sound must be bouncing off the cliffs around here," Al explained. "That river could be miles away."

For another hour or so they kept walking and tying string onto bushes. The water sound faded, too. Then, suddenly Scott stopped dead still.

"You guys aren't going to like this." Al poked his head around Scott's right shoulder while Benji peeked around his left side. What they saw would have made the bravest man sick. There, not more than ten feet ahead of them, a piece of white string flapped in the breeze.

"Hey, will you look at that," Benji said. "Somebody else is lost out here, too."

Scott and Al slowly turned to look at Benji.

"No, those are *our* strings! We've been walking around in one big circle for the last hour!" Scott groaned.

"Now what?" Al asked.

"You tell me."

"The sound! We forgot to follow the sound. The trail must take another fork someplace. We should follow our own strings, and arrows, and look for the cutoff."

That's what they did. Sure enough, there was a place where

the trail gave them two choices. The overgrown brush had hidden it from their view the first time around.

"It was a fork in the trail that got us into this mess in the first place," Al complained.

"You got a better suggestion?"

"No."

"All right then."

The boys pushed their way through the brush and continued walking. "It's going to get dark pretty soon. Isn't it?" Benji asked.

"Very good, Ben," Al mocked.

"You mean we're going to have to spend the night out here . . . *alone?*"

"No. We'll stop at the first hotel we see, Ben," Scott teased. "And I doubt we'll be alone. There are all kinds of critters living out here that would be more than happy to keep us company." The sound of rushing water now rumbled like constant thunder.

"We're getting closer," Al said.

The path began to open up slightly, and it was mostly dirt now. The boys approached two giant rocks, which stood like immovable sentries, guarding something just beyond. They walked between them, pushing the branches from tall saplings out of their way. As the boys emerged from the last remaining brush barrier, no one was prepared for what awaited them.

"What in the world is *that?*" Al cried out.

"It's a suspension bridge. You've seen them."

"You mean the kind that don't have any legs?" Benji asked. "Uh huh."

When they reached the bridge, the boys agreed that no one had crossed it in a long, long time. A large X had been tied across the entrance with heavy rope. Attached at the middle they found a metal sign, but the letters were all faded. Some of the paint had peeled away.

"A skull and cross bones," Benji said. "That's supposed to be bad, isn't it?"

"Cut it out Benji."

"Well, it is, and that's what's painted on the sign."

Scott wiped his hand across the sign's surface to reveal the word "DANGER" in big red letters. He grabbed one of the cable handrails and shook it. Fragments from the wooden cross-pieces broke loose and fell to the gorge below. That's when they looked down to see how deep it was.

Al whistled, "Man, that looks like the Grand Canyon."

"What are we going to do, Scott?" Benji asked in a whimper.

Chapter 7

The three boys looked out at the rickety, old bridge in front of them.

"Now what?" Al asked.

"Now, we try to get across," Scott said.

"Not me," Benji shouted. "I'm for turning around and following our strings right back to where we first came in."

"Aren't you forgetting something?"

"Oh, right. That bear thing."

"He should be long gone by now," Al suggested.

"Wanna bet?"

The boys knew that even crossing a suspension bridge in good condition can be a frightening experience. Not only can a person see off both sides, but the bridge reacts to the slightest movement. Wind can cause it to sway back and forth. This bridge presented those problems and a lot more.

Al took a long look at the crumbling bridge spanning what appeared to be a bottomless crack in the earth. "Got any ideas, Scott?"

"Just one."

"And?"

"We have to get across. That trail on the other side must lead someplace."

"Isn't that what you said about the trail that got us here?"

"It still makes sense. I mean, why would anyone go to all the trouble of building a bridge like this if it didn't go anyplace?"

"Oh, and it looks like people use this one *all* the time?"

"Anyone here afraid of heights?" Scott asked.

"Fortunately, no," they responded.

"Then, let's go."

"Wait a minute. Who goes first?" Benji asked.

Al had an idea. "We can draw straws for it." He reached down and picked a handful of weeds. From those he selected three stalks that looked similar. He kept one long, and broke the other two until he had shorter and shortest. After arranging them so all the tops looked equal, he held out his hand, "Draw."

Scott went first, "Mine looks middle-sized."

Then, Benji picked. "I got one longer than yours."

"Hey, no fair. It was my idea." Sure enough, Al was left with the shortest stalk.

"Batter up," Scott called.

"Let me hold your pack," Benji said.

"Nothin' doin'."

"I thought that if you go over the side, at least I'll have something to eat."

"Walk only on the support ropes. Don't trust any of the boards," Scott cautioned. Al inched his way out onto the bridge. He walked like one of those bowlegged cowboys after a long, hard ride. He moved first one leg and then the other. Once he was in the middle of the bridge, Scott couldn't hear Al's voice anymore, but he didn't know why. Just then a large section of rotten boards gave way. Like model hang-gliders they floated gently out of sight. The boys weren't sure where they went.

Scott was next. "Tell my mother I love her," he told Benji in a mocked cry. He, too, moved out onto the bridge. He noticed that the main suspension pieces were made of strong, braided, metal cables. He thought they must have been hanging there for a very long time because vines had overgrown them, and the few boards that remained attached to the bottom of the bridge were covered with a thick green moss.

"I don't think I like this," he called out.

"I didn't either," Al yelled from the other side.

"And I'm not planning to," Benji added.

When Scott reached the middle of the bridge, he understood why Al had had difficulty hearing. Directly beneath him, hundreds of feet down, the water rushed so hard over large rocks, it resembled a waterfall lying flat on the ground. *That looks really powerful*, he thought.

Eventually he reached Al on the other side. Now, it was Benji's turn.

"Go Benji, Go! Go Benji, Go! Go Benji, GO!" they chanted.

Benji held his arms in the air like a WWF champion. Then, he began his treacherous turn. He didn't have the weight of a backpack so that helped a little. But at the same time, his legs were the shortest. It became more difficult for his feet to reach the support ropes on both sides.

"I don't know if I can do this," he cried.

"Well, we aren't about to come back over," Al declared.

Cautiously, Benji inched his way along. The first part of the bridge was easy for him, but when he came to the middle . . . that part across the rushing whitewater . . . he slipped. Both feet went crashing through paper thin cross boards. Instinctively, he put his elbows out, and it's good that he did because that's the only thing that stopped him from plunging to the water and rocks below.

Horrified, Scott yelled, "Pull yourself up!" Then, the boys on the other side heard something that sounded like a guitar string just about to snap.

"Come on, Ben. The thing might fall!" Al warned. They didn't know for sure how he did it, but Benji managed to struggle back out of the hole he was in. The bridge leaned to one side from the strain of the weak support cable.

There were two more of those tell-tale warning sounds.

"You'd better hurry up, man," Scott warned. Somehow Benji got back to his feet and shuffled the rest of the way across to safety.

"Whew," he breathed heavily. "That was a close one."

"Yeah. That's enough of those for you, Ben."

"I know it, and I'm glad I didn't take your backpack. It would have been just enough weight to make me break through what few boards were keeping me up." That thought made him shake a little. "I was really scared."

After all the time it took them to get across, they now noticed that the sun was beginning to set.

"We'd better find a place to camp," Scott suggested. "There isn't time to cut branches for a shelter, and it looks to me like it might rain tonight."

"What do you think?" Al asked.

"I think we should try to find a place where we can get under a rock or something that's sticking out."

"What about a cave?"

"Don't know if we'd find one up here or not, but with the way these rocks look all pushed together we should find something."

For the next half-hour they searched until Benji called out, "What about that place?"

He had spotted an area big enough so they could all stay out of the weather. It was sort of like a cave but not really. There were tall, thick, rock walls on three sides with another flat piece of rock across the top that looked like a roof.

"I feel like the Flintstones in this place," Al said when they walked in.

"Quick. Let's get some dry wood before it gets totally dark,"

Scott said.

For the next few minutes they hurried to see what they could find.

"We need enough to last us the whole night," he reminded them. "Fire keeps the wild animals away."

"I'm all for that," Benji said. He worked even faster. Soon, it was time for them to put into practice another lesson they had learned in their survival class, building a fire.

Scott began digging a pit in the soft dirt. In the bottom he placed small pieces of tinder. He turned to Benji, "Give me the waterproof matches from your . . . pack."

Everyone sat silently.

"Um, I'm afraid Mr. Bear has those."

"Well, I can tell you one thing. If you guys think I'm going to try to make a hand drill, you're crazy," Al exclaimed.

"I always wondered if rubbing those sticks together really worked anyway," Benji scoffed. "Probably give you blisters."

"Then we're out of ideas," Scott sighed.

"Not necessarily," Al said slyly. "I brought my butane lighter, just in case."

"Some survival expert *you* turned out to be"

"Yeah, but I'll be the one with a fire tonight, that's for sure." He flipped the lighter causing a yellow and blue flame to burst out of the small opening at the top. Al touched its glowing flame to the tinder which burst into a warm, welcome, wonderful blaze. Quickly Scott built the teepee part of the fire over the flames and followed that with small logs as the fire grew.

"I'm glad we didn't lose your hatchet, Scott. We can cut all the logs we need with that baby."

In only minutes the boys were warming themselves in front of a delightful fire. Scott built it near the opening so they could sit safely behind its flames.

"It's a funny thing with fire," he said. "It's friendly to us but scary to the animals around us."

Benji moved a little closer to the flame, "I like being on the friendly side of it myself," he said with a nervous laugh.

They ate more trail mix quietly. Scott felt relieved that he had known what kind of shelter to look for and how to build a good fire. The part about not being prepared with matches bothered him though.

"What if something tries to get us?" Benji asked.

Al blurted out, "Ben, sometimes you drive a guy nuts. It wouldn't matter if it were cold or hot, raining or not, you'd still find something to worry about."

"That's okay, Al. Right now we could stand to worry a little more than usual. Absolutely no one knows where we are. No one! It's going to take everything we learned in survival class for us to have a chance to even make it out of this place."

"I know it will."

"So why don't we go over a couple things."

"Which things?" Benji asked.

"For one, we all need to get some sleep, but we don't dare

let our fire go out."

"Yeah, to keep those wild animals away," Al said, "like whatever it was that just made that noise."

Benji quivered. "I'll just pretend we didn't hear it."

"We *have* to hear it," Scott corrected. "We need to make sure we know everything we can out here. So, first let's check to see that we have plenty of wood for the fire."

Al held his hand out beyond the stone roof of their shelter. "Hey. I just felt some rain drops."

"I've never seen it so dark out either," Benji groaned. "We can't see more than about ten feet out there."

"Another reason for keeping the fire going. I'll use my hatchet to cut up the dead stuff. I think we should have enough firewood to make it till morning. Next, we have to set up guard duty."

"Guard duty?" Benji whined. "How does that work?"

"We each keep watch for like two hours. Then, you wake up the next guy so everyone sleeps some and guards some."

"What if, when it's my turn, something tries to get in here?" Benji asked.

"Then you'd better make more noise than you've ever made before in your whole life," Al said. "If something's gonna get me, I at least want to be awake when it happens."

"Nothing will get us, Al, but Ben, whoever is on guard has to wake the others so we can make noise, throw stuff, whatever we have to do to make it go away."

"Oh, man."

"So we'll take two hour turns. I'll go first, Al next, and Ben will go last. How does that sound?"

Al and Benji looked at each other, "Sounds good to us."

"We need to look out for snakes, too. They like to find warm places."

"Then they'll probably come in here by the hundreds to get next to our fire," Benji cried.

"It's too hot for them, just like it is for us. But you, in your sleeping bag, would be just about the right temperature. So be careful."

"I used to think I was safe in that thing," Benji complained. "Now, there's no place a guy can go, but at least I'm glad the bear didn't get that, too."

Al laughed. "I can see him squeezing into that bag right now. His mother probably told him, 'Breathe ten times and you'll be warm.'"

"You guys might as well get to bed." Scott looked at his watch. "My turn starts right . . . now." He pushed a button to begin the stopwatch function. Al and Benji went to their sleeping bags. They picked them up and began shaking them all around to make sure nothing could possibly be inside.

Benji was the last to climb in, "I should have gone on guard first because I don't think I can sleep one bit."

"That's okay. We can talk for awhile if you want," Scott suggested. "What if we played a riddle game?"

"Sure, what kind of riddle?"

"Can I play, too?" Al asked.

"You both can. The riddle is about a hanging bridge like the one we came across."

"Don't remind us," Benji shuddered.

"Here's the riddle. You're an explorer crossing a bridge like that, only it isn't falling apart. It's a strong one. The reason you're crossing it in the first place is because a bunch of bandits is chasing you."

"It was bad enough just making it across," Benji said.

"Well, this bridge doesn't have metal cables holding it up. It's made only out of wood and ropes. When you get to the middle of the bridge, you notice a second bunch of robbers coming toward you from the other end."

"I don't like this."

"Quiet, Ben, I do. What's next, Scott?"

"In your hands you have only two things: a hatchet. . . ."

"Is it an Estwing?" Benji interrupted.

"Sure, if you want it to be. You have that and a shotgun."

"I already know what I'd do," Al said.

"Wait, Al, there's a catch."

"What is it?"

"You have only one shell. Now, do you still think you know what to do?"

"Yeah, I'd try my best to wake up from this awful dream."

"Can't do that."

"Well, if I can't get out of it by waking up, then I'd take the hatchet and cut the bridge so no one could get me."

"How about you, Ben?"

"I'd take the shotgun and just start shooting up the place."

"With only one shell?" Al laughed.

"Oh . . . right."

"You guys got any other ideas?"

They thought for a minute, and then Benji said, "With the ones I think up, only part of them works."

"Well, so far neither of you has it right."

Then, Al got an idea. "I know. I'd . . . no, never mind. That wouldn't work either."

"So what would you do, Scott?"

"It's really not a fair question since I thought it up, but. . . ."

"No, wait, I think I got it," Benji shouted.

"Shoot."

"That's it. I'd take the one shell I had and put it in the shotgun. Right? Then, they don't know if I have one or a hundred."

"Good so far."

"Then, I'd aim it up in the air. Since people are running at me from both sides, I'd wait till they were almost on top of me."

"Yeah, but if you planned to crouch down at the last second, so they'd crash into each other, that wouldn't work because they'd just fall on you in a heap. Then what?" Al scoffed.

"Nope, I wouldn't crouch down. I'd wait till the very last second, and then raise my shotgun into the air, and fire off my one and only shell."

"That's the *stupidest* thing I ever heard. Isn't it stupid, Scott?"

"What next, Ben?"

"Well, everyone would stop dead in their tracks because they'd think they were next."

"Right."

"Then, I'd slowly lower my gun and motion for the bunch of guys blocking me from going the direction I wanted to go and make them squeeze by me and join the others."

"Right again. Then, what would you do?"

"I'd run like thunder to the other side."

"But then you'd have twice as many creeps after you, all coming from the same direction and no more bullets," Al told him.

"That's when I'd use my sharp hatchet. I'd cut the ropes so the bridge would start falling in, and all those guys would have to run to the other side. I'd be on the side of the river where I wanted to be, and they couldn't get me."

"Amazing, Ben. You worry so much before you have to take a test, but really you know a lot."

Benji yawned and stretched, "Yeah, but right now what I know is my brain wants to go to sleep."

"Mine, too. Keep all the monsters away from us, okay Scott?"

"I'll do my best."

"I can't ever remember being so tired," Benji mumbled

through a final yawn.

Al took out a laser pointer he'd brought along. He started shining it onto the rock that jutted out above their fire. Then, he moved its bright red beam around very fast, making a circle pattern on the rock.

"I didn't know you brought that thing," Scott said.

"You never know when you might want something like this on a camp out. We could use it to signal for help at night, I guess. Do you think anyone is looking for us by now?"

"I hope so, Al. I sure hope so."

"Me, too."

Chapter 8

Before long Scott heard the slow, even breathing of his friends. No one had spoken for several minutes so he figured they were finally asleep. He added a few more small logs to the fire and it flared up sending sparks dancing into the night air, giving off a little more light. For the first half-hour he seemed to notice every sound out in the darkness. He began wondering how many pairs of menacing eyes might be looking at him right now.

Man, he shuddered, *I don't like that idea at all.* So he quickly thought of something else. He thought about how much trouble they were going to be in for being so dumb.

What did we take that class for in the first place? he thought. He wondered if John and Brian were worried about him. *Brian is probably in as much trouble as we are*, he continued thinking.

Somehow his two hours passed a little more quickly than he had expected. Now, it was time to wake Al for his watch.

"Huh? What's happening? What's wrong?" Al asked in a sleepy voice.

"Your turn for guard duty. Sorry."

"That's okay. Anything happen?"

"Not much. There were a few sounds, but as long as the fire is going they seem to stay away."

"That's good. Two hours and then I wake Ben?"

"Yes."

"Okay, I'm up now. You'd better sleep some."

"Yeah, I'm dead."

Al took his place sitting on a rock that gave him a good view of their shelter. As far as Scott knew, in two hours Ben would be on guard, and then it would be his turn again. But things didn't work out exactly as he thought. In fact, the next thing he knew, he heard what sounded like a motor of some kind. *No, wait a minute*, he thought. *I hear TWO of them.*

Scott slowly opened his eyes. The first thing he noticed was the fire had gone completely cold. He looked over at the rock and saw that Ben was on guard duty. Well, he was in the place where he should have been watching, but he was asleep. The motors Scott heard actually were Benji and Al snoring.

"Ben, wake up!" he shouted.

"Huh, wha. . . .?"

"You fell asleep on guard."

"I did?"

"Yeah, you idiot."

"Hey, what's going on?" Al asked. "And what's that sound?"

No one was snoring now. "It's an airplane!" Scott yelled. The three boys rushed out of their shelter and began jumping up and down, screaming.

"Here! We're down here!" That's when Scott noticed that fog again covered the area of the mountain where they stood.

"I wonder if they're looking for us." Al asked.

"It won't much matter because if we can't see them. . . Well, you know the rest."

"Ben," Scott said, "you never should have let the fire go out."

"I couldn't help it; I was so tired."

"That's no excuse. We were all tired, but we had to take our turns."

"But I couldn't keep my eyes open."

"Then, you should have asked one of us."

"Well, you didn't tell us we could do that. Now did you?"

Scott took a deep breath. "We're up now. We can eat a little, and then we'd better get on the trail again." He noticed that the mood of his friends had changed from hope to fear. He knew it was up to him to change that. "As soon as we're packed, I'm sure we can find a way out of here. We just have to pull together."

That helped until Al asked, "How do we know we aren't walking farther and farther in the wrong direction, now that we're on the wrong side of the river?"

"We don't, but at least we know where we came from. There must be something at the other end of this trail. There just *has* to be."

"It could be that the closest place where people are is at the end of the trail we already came from," Al suggested.

"So, you're telling me you want to walk back across that broken-down bridge, and if that doesn't kill us, you'd like to go looking for the bear again?"

"Why do you keep reminding us of that bear?" Benji asked.

"Because we don't have any other choices."

"What about the part where you're supposed to stay put till help comes?" Al asked.

"That doesn't work anymore. We aren't in a place where people would *know* to search for us. Look at this trail. Nobody's walked on it for a long time," Scott said.

"And you still want to tell us we'll find something if we keep going?" Benji grumbled.

"Well, I'm open to all your suggestions, Ben." Benji didn't say another word.

"Follow me, then." Scott began to walk down the trail. Immediately he noticed something different. "You guys see what I see?"

"What?"

"The path is getting wider, and there aren't as many rocks to step on."

"Look up there," Benji pointed. "I think we won't have to climb as much up there." When they reached the place where he had pointed, the trail came to a flat area with sand. It felt good on their feet and made walking much easier.

"See, I told you things would get better," Scott said proudly.

It did look like the worst was finally behind them. The trail opened into a grassy meadow with wildflowers, trees, and a small stream running beside it.

Then, Al noticed something else. "Look over there." He pointed to some bushes with red and black berries.

"Are those what I *think* they are?"

"That depends on what you think they are," Scott laughed.

"Wild blackberries and red raspberries, that's what." He ran toward the bushes. When the others joined him, he was already eating berries as fast as he could pick them. "Mmmm. These are great," he managed to mumble as dark juice streamed down one corner of his mouth. Soon, the three boys had eaten all the sweet, juicy berries their stomachs could possibly hold.

"Ugh," Al grunted as he plopped down in the soft, green grass. "I think I could just about live here."

"Don't forget what they told us about the snow when we were in base camp. It probably gets even deeper up here."

"At least I could live here right now."

"I don't think people live anywhere near this place. It looks like a picture on a calendar or a magazine cover to me," Benji sighed. Then he collapsed onto the grass beside Al. "Too bad we can't pack up a bunch of these berries and take them with us."

"It sure beats trail mix," Al added.

Scott suddenly sniffed the cool mountain air like an old hound dog that knows a raccoon is hiding in a nearby tree. "You guys smell something?"

"Of course, we do," Al joked. "We've been out here on the trail for a couple days now. You can't expect us to smell very good."

"No. It isn't that. I think I smell smoke, like from a campfire."

"You mean there might be other campers around here?" Benji asked.

"What if we caught up with our group and just didn't know we were that close all the time?" Al suggested.

"I really miss the Timber Wolves," Benji said.

Al and Benji got to their feet and began to follow Scott who had already headed off in the direction where he thought the smoke might be coming from. They walked to the end of the meadow and entered a line of tall trees.

"It seems to be getting stronger," Scott said. Their dirt trail came to a spot where deep tire tracks went right through it. "Look! A car's been up here!"

"You mean like *that* one?" Al asked as he pointed toward another clump of bushes.

"Where?" Benji asked. "I don't see any car."

"Right there . . . behind all those branches. It's a great big truck"

"I think we should start yelling for help and see if someone comes" Benji suggested. "What do you think, Scott? Shouldn't we yell?"

"Wait a minute. Who parks their truck in the trees and then

covers it up with a bunch of branches?"

"Well, if you don't have a garage?" Benji said.

"Something doesn't feel right about this. Let's take a closer look."

Slowly they advanced toward the hidden truck. Scott reached in and moved branches to one side. "Look," Al said, "it's a rental." He pointed to a sticker on the bumper.

"This *is* strange," Scott whispered. "Here, cover it back up so no one will know we were here."

They quickly replaced the branches and then hid behind some big rocks to decide what they should do next.

"So what's the big problem, Scott?" Al asked.

"It seems to me they aren't just hiding their truck. It looks more like they don't want anyone to know they're here at all."

"How do you figure?"

"If a guy has a cabin up in the mountains, he might drive up there to spend a few days. He might even park his truck in some trees. But I doubt that any normal person is going to take the time to chop down a bunch of branches and completely cover the thing up. I say there could be something going on here that shouldn't be."

"Why don't we sneak around and get a better look?" Al suggested. "Let's leave our backpacks behind these rocks."

Cautiously the boys followed another set of tire tracks pressed down in the dirt. "These look pretty fresh," Scott whispered. They crawled up behind a line of bushes and stopped.

Al reached up and pushed them apart. "Hey, looks like an abandoned cabin," Benji whispered, "and the place could use a little work."

"It can't be abandoned," Al said. "There's smoke coming out of the chimney."

The roof had wood shingles covered with thick green moss, like on the old bridge they had crossed. Water from years of rain and snow had rotted through part of one wall.

Scott noticed several windows were cracked or broken. "I think we should wait around until dark so we can get in closer."

"Are you crazy?" Benji demanded. "I'm not spending another night sleeping outside. No sir! Not me!"

"Keep your voice down," Scott warned.

"Well, I'm not," he whispered, "and that's all there is to it."

"You mean like you slept last night when you were supposed to be guarding us," Al said.

"Let's stay here for awhile and see if anyone comes out," Benji suggested.

"I'm for taking a look," Al said.

"Whatever makes you happy," Benji scoffed.

"What do you think, Scott?"

"Well, maybe one person could sneak up, look in, and get back here easier than all three of us. But you *have* to be careful."

"I will."

"And don't let anyone see you." Benji added.

"I won't." Al whispered.

With that, Al darted from tree to tree until he was only a few feet from the cabin. He crept up to a side window and peered in. Scott and Benji watched as their friend took one look inside, dropped to the ground, then, ran back to them as fast as they had ever seen him run.

Scott noticed the frightened look on Al's face. "What's wrong?"

"Yeah," Benji added. "What'd you see in there?"

It took a few moments for Al to calm down. He was breathing heavily. Then he said, "Give me a drink of water . . . quick!" After a couple of swallows he said, "I'm not sure *what* I saw, but I think it's bad."

"Bad? Like what?" Benji asked.

Al shook his head. "I'm not really sure. I think you guys better see for yourselves."

"Well, we can't go right away. We have to be sure no one saw you," Scott warned.

For about a half-hour they watched and waited, but nothing happened. The smoke continued rising steadily from the crumbled chimney. It gave off a sweet smell that reminded Scott of burning pine branches in his fireplace back home at Christmas time. Right then he wished he could be back there again, safe.

"I think we can sneak up and take a look through the window there at the back, but that's it. Then, we're out of here," Scott said.

Like secret commandos, the boys slinked down behind the bushes. They began moving from rock to rock, behind trees, under bushes, until they were crouched next to an old wooden shed.

"Just a quick look from the porch over there and then we get back right away," Scott ordered. They stepped quietly onto the old boards and moved up to the window.

Benji was too short. "I can't see in," he complained. While Scott and Al peered in through the dirty windows, Benji found an old rusty bucket in the corner. He picked it up, brought it to the window, turned it upside down and began stepping up for a chance to look in. As he did that, he lost his balance and went crashing onto the old boards, rotted leaves, and branches that had also fallen there over time.

Scott didn't know where the sound had come from because he was intent on what he saw inside. He and Al turned and ran away as fast as they could go, but Benji had gotten one of his feet tangled in the bucket's handle when he fell. "Hey, you guys. Help me, will ya?"

His friends dove under some bushes and rolled to a stop. When they looked back, they saw something almost too terrible to describe. Two scary looking men who must have been inside the cabin now held Benji by both arms and they were dragging him back toward the open door.

Both men were big and strong. They wore dark clothes and dirty black boots. Benji didn't have a chance.

"Help! Somebody help me!" Benji screamed frantically.

Scott knew because of what he had seen inside that place, he was not about to move a muscle.

"Did you see the same thing I saw in there?" Al whispered.

"I sure did."

"What do you think we should do? I mean, we can't just leave him here."

"Well, we can't go back there now. Those guys'll catch us too. I don't think they'd like it if anyone knew what they were up to."

"Help, please, help," Benji continued yelling, but he was already inside the cabin. His voice became distant and muffled. Then, the door slammed shut.

"I need to think," Scott groaned. "We have to get him out of that place, and I mean fast, or else."

Chapter 9

Scott needed time to come up with a plan all right. It had to be more than just what to do now. He also had to think through what he and Al had seen inside the abandoned cabin that wasn't so abandoned.

"Who do you think those guys are?" Al asked.

"At first I thought they were poachers like I've read about."

"What are poachers?"

They trap animals and sell them or their skins for a lot of money."

"But what did you think of all those maps on the walls?" Al asked.

"Those bothered me a lot, but I saw something else that gave me goose bumps all over."

"What? I didn't see anything else."

"I did. They were like pictures I've seen before. One time I was messing around with my computer, and I stumbled onto a site that offered pictures you could buy if you had a credit card."

"I didn't see any pictures in there."

"You saw them. You just didn't know what you were looking at."

"What were they?" Al asked.

"Satellite pictures. The place I found on the Internet was a company that sells them."

"Satellite pictures? Of what?"

"They're shot from out in space. You can buy pictures that show the block you live on, or even your own house if you knew how to order them."

"No kidding?"

"Yes. Companies like to have a picture of their office buildings or a developer might want to show off a neighborhood he built. I've even seen some of the video used in a couple of commercials."

"You saw pictures like that in the cabin?"

"Yes . . . buildings. I saw lots of buildings."

"What else?"

"Pictures of a power generator and a huge refinery."

"I don't know why anyone would want pictures like that in a cabin way up here."

"Me either, but it can't be good."

"Well, we have to get Ben. We just have to," Al groaned.

"After dark, I want to take a second look inside the cabin," Scott replied.

"Are you nuts?"

"I wonder that too sometimes," Scott joked, "but we have to

be sure what we're dealing with before we go off and report these guys. I mean, we could be wrong."

"And if you're sure?"

"I have an idea, but we have to wait till dark."

"Then what?"

"You still got that laser pointer on you?"

Al felt around in his pockets. "It should be here someplace. Yeah, here it is."

"Good. Do you have your camera?"

"I do, but it's in my backpack."

"Well, we need that, too. Let's go get it. We can talk more over there."

The boys crawled carefully back toward the rocks where they had hidden their things.

Scott pointed, "There they are."

Al went to his pack, reached in, and pulled out the camera. "Do we need anything else?"

"Your lighter. If those guys are what I think they are, it wouldn't hurt to pray, too."

"You mean out loud?" Al asked.

"It doesn't have to be, but let's just make sure we do it. I know I will be!"

"So will I. What's the plan?"

"After it gets real dark, we'll build a big fire over by their truck so after we light it they'll see it and think it's on fire. We need to flatten all their tires, too, so they can't drive away."

"I like that idea."

"After we get the fire going, we'll have to run back to a window on each side of the cabin. You'll have your camera with you at one window, and I'll take the laser with me to the other. Everything we do has to be timed exactly."

"I don't get it."

"Haven't you seen those movies where high-powered rifles have a red laser sight?"

"Oh, yeah. Now, I see. You're going to shine my pointer in through the window and they'll think they're about to be attacked."

"Right."

"But what's my camera for?"

"It's just to confuse them. When you first see me turn on the laser, you count to ten. Then start shooting off your flash as many times as you can while you count to ten again."

"I can set it for rapid fire."

"Great."

"Then what?"

"I think they'll be so scared by what they *think* is happening, they'll all come running out of that place."

"Then they see the fire?"

Scott nodded. "If they think it's their truck going up in flames and that's their only way of getting out of here, everyone in the cabin is going to be very upset. They should forget all about our little Benny just long enough so we can get him out of there, run into the woods, and hide. We'll put our backpacks in a new place where we can find them when we come out."

The boys checked out the laser and flash to make sure they worked. Al tested his lighter. Right then, Scott was glad his friend didn't stick with bringing only the survival things that were on the list.

They worried about how Benji was doing inside, but there wasn't anything they could do for him right away. Before long the sun went down and the sky turned from orange and red to black with stars. The stars shined brightly, but there was no moon in the clear sky.

Before acting on their plan, the boys needed to be sure it was the right thing to do. The only way to know meant they had to go back to the same dirty windows on the same rotted porch and look in again.

In the darkness they crept toward the cabin. An eerie light from a lantern shone out between pieces of cloth that partly covered the inside of the windows.

Scott peered in, and this time he was sure of what he saw. The pictures could have only one purpose. His heart began to pound rapidly as his whole body went cold.

"This is bad, Al, real bad," he whispered.

Then, both boys saw Benji sitting in a wooden chair sound asleep.

"That kid can sleep anywhere," Al complained.

"Let's get away from here," Scott warned.

Together they moved back into the safety of the bushes and surrounding darkness.

"Who are those guys?" Al asked.

"I'm not exactly sure, but you know how we're supposed to keep our eyes open for things that don't look right?"

"Are you talking about. . . ?"

"Terrorists? Yes, and that's who I think they are."

"How come?"

"Because of how they're hiding . . . especially because of the maps and satellite pictures."

"But they could be developers . . . or looking for oil."

Scott shook his head. "I don't think so."

"Why not?"

"They would never have grabbed Ben unless they were up to something bad. Now, let's get started."

Quietly the boys began gathering sticks and dead wood. Because the night was so dark, they had to feel around in the dirt until they found enough for their fire.

"You know what to do?" Scott asked.

"Wait until I see the laser, count to ten, then flash my camera while I'm counting to ten again. Then, we run in and get Ben."

"It's a good thing we learned about making a fire," Al whispered as they stacked the last few logs into a teepee shape.

"That looks good. Light it Al, and let's get in position."

Al lit the fire then quickly moved to a window close by while

Scott darted around to the other side of the cabin. When he looked in, he saw the four men taking their maps and pictures off the walls. Scott thought they looked nervous. He could hear them talking, but it wasn't in English. He couldn't make out what language they were speaking.

He could see Benji in the middle of the room. The men had wrapped strong wide tape around his chest and arms and the chair. He was taped to the chair!

Scott felt nervous and unsure if his plan would work. His mouth went dry as a sick feeling made his stomach churn. His hands were so cold and clammy the laser pointer almost slipped from his fingers.

He hoped Al could remember to do his part on time. He didn't know if the men would do what he expected, and he wasn't sure if he could save Benji. *But I'm willing to do whatever I can to save my friend*, he thought. Then, he remembered something he'd heard in Sunday school. It was a story about a man being willing to die for his friend. *Not sure if I'm ready to go that far*, he thought.

Scott took three deep breaths.

He glanced around the room one more time. Most of the pictures and maps had been taken from the walls. Scott saw several of them rolled up on a table. Then, he aimed his laser beam through the window. It shot across the room blasting its intense, focused, red dot of light onto the wall next to one of the men. Right away one of the others saw it and cried out in terror.

Scott had never heard such fear come out of the mouth of

anyone before.

He quickly moved the laser until it landed right in the center of the forehead of the meanest looking man in the room.

That man couldn't see the light, but the others did. Scott held it as steady as he could so it stayed right on the man's head. The others became frantic. They all began screaming and running around inside the cabin. Everything happened so fast.

The man with the red laser dot on his forehead turned to see his reflection in a large mirror on an opposite wall. At that same instant, Al started shooting off his flash as fast as it would recharge and fire. The beam hit another smaller mirror so light ricocheted from several directions. Scott hadn't planned for that, but he was glad it happened.

Just as he suspected, the men dashed through the front door and ran into the night. It was at that point one of them saw the fire and began yelling some kind of warning at the top of this voice. All four rushed toward the fire.

Scott and Al burst into the cabin to get Benji. "We don't have time to cut the tape, Ben. You're gonna have to get out of here while you're still stuck to the chair."

Scott was able to get a close-up look at the maps and pictures. Now, there was no doubt.

They helped Benji onto his feet and moved toward the door. He looked like something out of a monster movie. All hunched over, he lumbered across the floor. "I thought I was never going to see you guys again."

"Quiet till we get away from this place," Scott whispered.

The boys hurried out of the cabin, scooped up their back-packs, and headed deeper into the dark woods. Only after they were at a safe enough distance, Scott told them to stop so he could free his friend from the chair.

"Thanks, you guys. It feels so good to get that stuff off me. It made my skin itch."

"We're just glad to get you out of there," Al told him.

"Who were those guys anyway?" Benji asked.

"I'm not sure," Scott said.

"While I was in there, I saw them talking on one of those satellite phones."

"You mean a cell phone?"

"No. It was bigger than that. Didn't the brochure tell us not to bring our cell phones along because they'd be useless?"

"That's right," Al answered. "There aren't any towers up here."

"We should still call 911 or something," Benji said.

In a disgusted voice Scott snapped, "Sure, Ben. We'll just stop at the next pay phone we find hanging from a tree."

"Well, we should do something. That's all."

"What we're *going* to do is try and find a safe place where we can stay until morning. Then, we have to get off this mountain, find help, and tell somebody what we saw."

"But what about a shelter?" Al asked.

"And a fire?" Benji added.

"Can't take the chance. We're gonna have to rough it out-side in the dark and the cold. That's why we took the class . . . for something just like this."

Not another word was spoken as the boys tried to find their way in the dark. At least the sky was still clear. Even without a moon, the stars gave off just enough light so they could see as they put one foot in front of the other. After a few more steps, Scott held up his hand. "Stop. This looks like a good place."

"I think we should go on a little farther," Benji said.

"No, we stop here. Lay out your sleeping bags, and we'll put our waterproof tarps on top in case it rains."

Scott had found a place that was slightly hidden from view by some boulders that formed a barrier between where they were and the cabin. In near total darkness they passed around bags of trail mix. At that moment, for some reason, it tasted the best they could remember on the whole trip.

"What about guard duty?" Al asked.

"Yes, we need to do that again, but we can't have a fire."

"Man, you mean we're just going to lay around out here and wait for something to eat us?" Benji groaned.

Al reminded him, "Don't forget, you're the guy who fell asleep last time."

"It won't happen tonight. I promise."

"Al, you go first, and Ben, you'll be second, then me. We'll use your laser and flash it if anyone hears the slightest noise."

Al sat on top of his bed while the others climbed into their sleeping bags.

"I'm cold," Benji complained, "but I remember . . . breathe ten times."

"You're learning," Scott said.

In a muffled voice from inside the bag, Scott heard Benji say, "Hey, Scott?"

"Yes?"

"Thanks for getting me out of that place. I think they were getting ready to leave pretty soon."

"What makes you think that?"

"Because they had already packed all their clothes into duffel bags, and they also got a bunch of calls real close together. The big, mean-looking guy . . . remember him?"

"I thought they all looked mean."

"Yeah, wait till you see the pictures I took back there."

"Well, that biggest one got *real* nervous, and he kept looking at me like he was planning to do something. He tried to ask me questions, only I couldn't understand most of it." Benji thought for a moment. "I wouldn't have told them anything though."

"I'm glad nothing happened to you, Ben."

"Me, too."

"Now, I just hope we can find some help in the morning."

"I'd be happy if we even get to see another morning"

"Did you have to say that?" Al groaned.

Chapter 10

As the sun began to rise, Benji was on guard, and he was awake this time. Even though it had rained in the night, he continued sitting on top of a big rock with his back toward the sunrise and a tarp over his head.

Cold, damp air surrounding the boys caused their joints to feel stiff and sore.

The early daylight made Scott wake up, and he saw that Al was starting to move, too.

"Man, I hurt everywhere," Al complained.

Scott looked to see if Benji was guarding like he promised. Then, he noticed something that scared him so bad he couldn't breathe for a moment.

"Al," he gasped. "Look!"

He pointed behind where Benji was perched up on top of a big slippery rock.

"Don't turn around, Ben," Al warned.

"Why not?" he whispered.

"Because you are not going to like what you see right

behind you."

"Not those guys again?" he begged. Then, he raised his arms to surrender.

Scott slipped out of his sleeping bag to go over and help his friend who was unaware of the danger less than a foot behind where he sat.

"Take my hand," Scott ordered. By then Al was at Scott's side and took Benji's other hand.

"Now, ease yourself off the rock," Scott said.

As Benji did that, he turned around to see what all the fuss was about. That's when he had a clear view of what his friends had already seen. All three boys had taken their turns sitting on the same rock during the night in total darkness with no idea of the danger only inches away.

Benji slid down off the rock. "I feel dizzy," he groaned. The boys had been sitting in the dark next to a sheer cliff the entire night.

"That thing goes down a lot farther than where we crossed the bridge," Scott shuddered hoarsely.

"Ben, weren't you the one who said, 'I think we should go on a little farther?' Good thing we didn't listen to you. Just two more steps and wham-o! We'd have bounced off the side of the cliff like three beach balls . . . all the way to the bottom."

"Yeah! Thanks for ignoring me this time. What do we do now?"

"We can't go near that cabin," Scott said.

"Why not? They should be gone by now," Benji suggested.

"Not with what we did to their tires," Al said.

"Did you flatten them?"

"Like pancakes . . . while you were tied up."

"What a great idea. You should get a medal or something. Only that means they can't drive away, and that also means they must still be around here someplace." Benji scanned the area nervously.

"We should start walking, and see if we can find help," Scott said.

Then, he began leading them on another trail that sloped downward along the top of the steep cliff they had just discovered. "Be careful. That first step is a *killer*," he joked as he looked over the side.

"Wait. I hear something again," Benji whispered.

"It's another plane. No, I hear two of them," Al added.

Scott was already reaching into his pack. "Get out your signal mirrors." The sun wasn't fully up in the sky so it was impossible to get any bright reflection for a signal. "Forget that. We need to make one of those distress signs. Quick, get all the long dead wood you can find. Hurry!"

They rushed into the trees and brought out several branches. Scott made three signs. First, he arranged logs into one letter V on top of another just like it. "There, that ought to get somebody."

"Did you mean to make the 'we need firearms and

ammunition' one?" Al asked. "That's dumb. You know they aren't going to give those to a bunch of kids our age."

"I know. Now help me with the next one." He rolled the biggest single log he could find, out into the middle of the area. "We don't need a doctor," Benji said.

Next, he made the letter F out of the remaining logs so it would look like they also needed food and water. "There. Now anyone who sees that we need all these things is going to know something's up."

Al and Benji smiled at each other. "What's the sign for 'I want my mommy?'" Benji laughed.

"Next, we have to lay flat on the ground."

"Why not stand up and wave our arms?" Al asked.

"Don't you remember? From the air, all they would be looking at is the tops of our heads, which will look pretty small from way up there. Now lie down."

They lay on the rocks as Scott instructed. He looked over to his friends and knew their blue jeans, along with their red, yellow, and blue jackets, would stand out against the dark, gray rocks. The two planes they could only hear earlier, now banked toward their direction and passed right over where they were.

"I think they saw us," Benji yelled.

"Keep your voice down." The planes quickly disappeared over the next ridge.

"I don't think they saw us," Benji moaned.

Scott looked at his watch. It was only six in the morning.

"They probably only had sightseers in them anyway. Come on. We'd better hurry."

They turned to walk down the path again when the oddest thing happened.

"Hey, Scott," Al whispered. "Notice anything strange about the bushes around here?"

"Looks like somebody just planted them," Benji said out of one side of his mouth. As soon as he said that, bushes all around them rustled a little. Then, the bushes rose higher!

"Hey, they have feet," Benji whispered, "and guns!"

"Just keep walking, stare straight ahead, and don't look at them," Scott ordered.

That's when more soldiers than the boys had ever seen before, even in a Fourth of July parade, moved toward them.

"We're surrounded," Benji cried.

At that moment, a very important looking man walked out from behind some of the large rocks. He didn't have any bushes anyplace on his helmet or uniform.

"My name is Colonel Stone. This is Captain Ward, and Sergeant Reid. Who are you?"

"I'm Scott. These are my friends, Ben, and Al.," he answered in a trembling voice.

"What are you boys doing in this area?"

"We got lost."

"Where are you supposed to be?"

"We started out on a Wilderness Wanderers campout."

"Yeah," Al added. "We were Timber Wolves, but we lost the rest of our group in the fog a couple days ago."

"We've seen your pictures. You boys are all on the news back in Denver . . . probably around the world on those cable news programs, too."

"We are?" Al asked.

"Yes. There are search planes looking for you all over these mountains."

"There are?" the boys asked together.

"Did you know you're in a restricted military zone right now?"

"No, sir," Scott answered.

"Well, you are. There isn't supposed to be anyone up here. We're conducting mountain training exercises on a search and capture mission."

"That explains it then. You must be looking for those guys in the cabin. Right?"

"We came over here because our spotters saw a big fire last night."

"We did that," Scott told him.

"What guys are you talking about?"

Benji couldn't help laughing. "They look really real. They're all dressed like terrorists. Boy, oh, boy, they sure had me scared."

"Yeah," Al added, "and they had maps and satellite pictures all over their walls."

"I saw them, too," Scott told him, "but they packed those

all up."

The colonel took a map from a pocket in his uniform. "Sergeant, get on the radio, ASAP. Tell the red team to join us at these coordinates, here." He pointed to a black square spot on his large green map. "Order them to break off from the exercises. Tell them this is not a drill." The colonel led everyone straight back up the hill, to the woods by the old abandoned cabin. In minutes they were joined by another group of soldiers just as big as the first.

"You boys stay behind these rocks," the colonel ordered.

He immediately gave instructions to his men, and they moved into positions surrounding the cabin. The colonel took a loud bullhorn and ordered, "You, in the cabin. Come out with your hands in the air. This is the U. S. Army. You are completely surrounded."

"Probably they're still sleeping," Al said. "We scared them pretty good last night."

The colonel repeated his warning, but no one came out.

"Tear gas!" the colonel barked.

Quickly three soldiers took up closer positions around the cabin.

Then, another officer gave the command, "Fire!"

Tear gas canisters crashed through the windows into the cabin. Nothing happened for a few seconds. Then, slowly, white smoke drifted out from the broken windows.

A slight breeze blew a little of the smoke back toward where the boys were standing. Immediately, Scott's eyes started burning. Tears flowed down his cheeks. He noticed that Al and Benji were having the same problem. When he looked up through his blurry eyes, all the soldiers had put on gas masks.

"Prepare to storm the cabin," the colonel ordered.

By now the boys were coughing and sneezing like they were standing in the middle of a ragweed patch with severe allergies.

"Man," Al choked, "if it's this bad out here, it must be awful for those guys inside."

"Maybe they're already gone," Scott suggested.

The soldiers prepared to make their final assault when the front door to the cabin flew open as four men burst out with their hands raised into the air. Like the boys, they were coughing, sneezing, and crying. They were quickly captured and taken away.

"Sir," Scott heard one of the soldiers call out. "You gotta see this."

He began to pull a few branches away from the hidden truck. There it sat with all four tires still completely flat.

"Bring those boys over here."

Scott, Benji, and Al were brought to where he was standing. "Any possibility you boys are responsible for this?" he asked in a gruff voice.

"Are we in trouble if we did?" Benji asked.

"No."

"Then we did it."

"Outstanding! First rate work." He ambled back toward the cabin, and as he walked away he bellowed, "You boys deserve medals or something. Flat tires. Who would have thought of that?" He just kept laughing.

Scott and his friends were taken back to the place where they had first seen the soldiers and had dropped their backpacks.

"Get your gear together," a soldier instructed. "You'll be moving out soon."

The boys were picking up their sleeping bags, tarps, and backpacks when Al heard something. "Hey, what's that noise?"

"Sounds like a helicopter to me," Scott said. They turned in the direction of the steep cliff and looked up into the sky, thinking it might be about to fly past them. The sound got louder and louder, but still they couldn't see anything. Suddenly, just the main rotor blade emerged . . . not from above them but from below. Like a giant bird it cleared the top of the cliff, went high over their heads, and then began descending right toward them.

Scott looked over his shoulder and noticed another soldier making signals to the pilot with his arms.

"Hey, you guys, that thing's going to land up here!" Al exclaimed.

The huge blades from the chopper cracked through the air creating shock waves that made a pop, pop, pop, pop sound. As it came closer to the ground, dirt from the area blew around like a desert sandstorm.

Scott squinted until his eyes were only small slits. He didn't want to miss a thing. "I've never seen one of those close up. This is great!"

The helicopter gently touched down on a huge flat rock surface and soon the blades slowed to a stop.

"I wonder what it's up here for," Benji asked.

"Probably to take those guys from the cabin off to jail," Al suggested.

"Man, oh, man. I sure wish we could take a ride in that thing," Scott exclaimed.

"That would never happen," Al said, "Would it?"

Chapter 11

It seemed to Scott like they had been waiting on the rocks for a long time, but he kept looking at his watch. It had only been about an hour. Then, almost as abruptly as the soldiers had appeared in the first place, the colonel came storming back out through the bushes. He walked straight up to where the boys were sitting, so they stood up to meet him.

"Come on. Let's get in. Time's a wastin'," he barked. Two other soldiers walked to the helicopter and slid open the large doors on each side.

"What happened to those men?" Al asked. "We thought the helicopter was for them."

"Ha! Not likely. Letting those guys ride in my helicopter would be too good for them. They're the worst kind of people, son."

"So what happened to them? You didn't. . . ?" Benji asked.

"Didn't what?"

"You know."

"Of course not. I've got about two thousand men up here in

these mountains today. We had a big operation planned but nothing like what you boys turned up for us. We've got a lockup area down at the battalion's base camp. They'll be taken there first then turned over to the proper authorities."

Scott could hardly believe it as he and his friends got to climb up into the helicopter and find their seats. A high-pitched whining sound gradually began, followed by the roar of a large jet engine. Those huge blades turned, first slowly, then faster, and faster. Soldiers made sure each boy had his seat belt on as tightly as possible. Then a big green helmet was placed on each of their heads. Black wires were attached to the back of each helmet, and each had a microphone in the front.

Scott watched as the colonel put on his own helmet and connected the wire. Then he flipped a switch and asked, "Doors open or closed?"

"Open," they all yelled.

"You have to push that switch if you want to talk."

They did that, and then all at once yelled again, "OPEN."

That made the colonel shake his head like he was in pain.

Scott pushed his talk button again, "Why didn't you fly those guys down with us?"

"They're extremely dangerous men, for one thing, and I'm sure they aren't too happy with you boys since you uncovered what they were doing. But actually, I don't think they'd be very welcome where we're going."

Wonder what that meant? Scott thought.

Al pushed his talk button. "So where are we going?"

"You'll see. Pilot?"

"Yes, sir."

"Take'er up."

"Sir!"

The blades turned even faster now as the engine grew louder. In seconds the helicopter lifted up only a few feet off the ground. Scott leaned his head slightly outside the door so he could look down. Immediately, those shock waves he had only heard before now bounced off the top of his helmet with such force he felt like his head was under a giant, hungry woodpecker.

The helicopter lifted a little higher; then it turned completely around in the opposite direction. Scott had been on a few airplanes before . . . everything from a jumbo jet to a small private airplane, but the sounds on this ride were completely different. It felt funny to be sitting in one spot and still be up in the air at the same time. He thought it would be hard to describe to anyone who had never done it before.

While he was thinking about that, the nose of the helicopter dipped down slightly, and then it moved forward like one of those drag racers he'd seen on TV. He listened as the pilot talked to someone on the radio. They used a few regular words and some numbers. It sounded like a code to him. When the pilot stopped talking, Scott pushed his talk switch and said to his friends, "What do you guys think? Is this the coolest thing you've ever done or what?"

"We do this everyday," a voice crackled from up front.

Now Scott was embarrassed. He'd forgotten that everyone else in the helicopter could hear him, too.

Then the same voice came back on, "I'm just kidding you boys. Hi, my name is Dan. What's yours?"

"I'm Al"

"Mine's Benji, I mean, Ben."

"And I'm Scott."

"Well, pleased to have such celebrities aboard my ship. Up to now, the most important person I've ever flown was a United States Senator."

Hearing that, the colonel pushed his talk button and cleared his throat loudly.

"Oh, and the good colonel there, too, of course."

"That's better," the grumpy-sounding officer responded.

"Did you know you were so famous, Scott?" the pilot asked.

"No, we didn't. I mean, we are?"

"You sure are. I need to warn you about what's going to happen down below."

"What?" Scott questioned.

"Search teams have been combing these mountains for the last couple days. You know how the twenty-four-hour news channels are. They have to fill all those hours with something."

"I know. My parents hate that, when some of the stories go on and on," Benji said.

The colonel came on the headset. "Well, the story of three

boys lost in the Rocky Mountains is big enough by itself. There have been television satellite trucks, radio stations, and newspaper people flocking to this area."

"Really?" Al asked.

"Yes, and that's before the really *big* story hit."

"The *big* story?" Al repeated.

"They've already gotten the reports of exactly what you uncovered up here."

"And *exactly* what was that?" Scott asked. "I mean, I saw the maps, and I knew about satellite pictures taken from space."

"Ever since what happened in New York and DC, you've probably heard about something they call 'sleeper cells' that might still be in our country."

"I think so," Scott said, "but I don't know if we understand what that is."

Dan came on the headset. "They're people who live here and are just waiting for the signal to do as much damage as they can."

"That's right," the colonel added. "Your mountain buddies were planning to hit some pretty important targets around the city of Denver. You boys stopped that from happening. I'm telling you, it's a really big story."

"But we were lost. We didn't really *do* anything."

"There's where you're wrong. You were smart enough to let the air out of their tires. From what we could tell, they were packed up and ready to go. When they found the tires were flat, they called for help."

"I'm glad we did that," Scott said proudly.

"But there's one thing that still puzzles me," the colonel continued.

"What's that?" Scott asked.

"We intercepted some of their communications. Do you know anything about a high-powered weapon with a laser sight?"

All three boys laughed as Al reached into his pocket and pulled out his harmless laser pointer. He pressed the button and asked, "You mean like this?"

The colonel had laughed pretty hard about the flat tires but when he saw Al's innocent little pointer, he began laughing uncontrollably. That made him cough and choke until his eyes ran with tears like the boys' eyes had run from the tear gas.

Finally, he regained control of himself and breathed deeply. Then he let out a long sigh.

"They had one of those satellite phones, too," Benji recalled.

"I know they did," the colonel said, taking another deep breath, "and we have the ability to track where the calls were made. Right now, as we're flying to the circus below, the FBI should be knocking on a few doors someplace and arresting even more people. So, you did do something very important."

"Unbelievable," Scott whispered. When he looked out the side of the helicopter, he began to get an idea of what the colonel was talking about and why he said "circus." Below them he saw so many people that it looked like, well, a circus. In minutes they were touching down in a large grassy spot.

"I see my parents," Scott yelled. "Yours, too, Al, and there are your mom and dad, Ben."

A very important looking man approached the door as the engine and blades slowed down. He wore a dark suit with a red and blue-striped tie. Scott wondered how his black shoes could be so clean and shiny up here at the foot of the mountains. Even at a distance, photographers and videographers had already begun taking pictures.

"Helmets off, boys," Dan instructed.

And I thought they might have been poachers, Scott thought. *This is bigger than any poachers . . . a lot bigger.* He could see some kind of a platform that had been set up in the center of the flat, grassy area. There were rails on all sides so people wouldn't fall off and there were steps on one side. He could also see a podium with a microphone. Speakers had been put up high on poles to help all the people hear what would be said. The important-looking man gave instructions about what to expect.

"I'm the Governor of Colorado. I'll take you up on the stage where we have some chairs for you. A lot of people want to say a few words. There will be presentations and one of you needs to be selected to speak."

The boys got together and talked it over. "I think it should be Scott," Al began. "He was our leader."

"Some leader I turned out to be. As far as I'm concerned, I did the wrong thing at every turn."

"Yeah, but it was your plan to get Ben out that did it . . . that and thinking about the tires."

"You heard what the army guy said about that part," Benji added.

"Thanks, guys, but I want it to be Ben who gets to talk. He's the one that had to stay in the cabin with those terrible men. Who knows what could have happened?"

Al put his hand on Benji's shoulder. "Then, it's settled."

"Me? Are you sure?"

"We're sure."

"Man, I'm *so* scared."

"So, that's supposed to be different?" Al joked.

The governor had been right. There were a lot of people who seemed to think they had something important to say. That part went on and on. Next, the boys were asked to come to the front of the stage. Another very important-looking man approached them. He had three shiny medals in his hand attached to red, white, and blue ribbons. He also wore a small radio earpiece.

"On behalf of the President of The United States of America, I present you with this medal signifying your bravery, honor, and love for America. Thank you." He shook hands with each of the boys.

"You saw a situation that didn't look right. You took action and did something about it. The President is asking all of us to be on the lookout. You brave, young men have shown the nation what can happen when we do that, and we're grateful. You are true patriots."

Each boy had one of the medals placed around his neck as the crowd applauded. Then Benji was invited to speak. Timidly, he walked toward the microphone. Someone had to bring a box for him to stand on so the crowd could see him over the top of the podium.

"Hi. My name's Benj . . . Ben, and I'm a little nervous."

The crowd laughed.

"These are my very best friends, Scott and Al."

A loud cheer erupted for the boys.

"When we got lost out there, we knew we were in real trouble. I thought when the bear almost got me . . . well, that was bad."

His mother shrieked and almost fainted. Benji's father had to hold on to her tightly.

"But then when I nearly fell through that broken down old bridge over the canyon that we couldn't see the bottom of . . . that was bad, too." Benji's father motioned for one of the medical people to give him a hand.

"Then, when those big, mean guys caught me and tied me up in their cabin . . . that was bad." Now Benji's father was looking a little pale.

"And this morning, when Scott woke up and showed me I'd been sitting in the dark just two inches from a drop off that I also couldn't see the bottom of, whew, that could have been really bad."

His parents could no longer stand up under their own power. Weak in the knees, they both had to sit on the ground. Actually, if his mother wasn't leaning on her husband, she would have been flat out on the grass. A nurse began to revive her.

"I guess the worst thing is what could have happened if we hadn't run into the army up there, and those guys had gotten away. Man, that could have been really, really bad. So we're just glad to be back down here, safe. Thank you."

Again the people cheered for them. It wasn't long before they all left the platform, and two of the boys were able to join their parents immediately. All three were interviewed by the national television and radio reporters. When that was finished, Benji's mother looked around and asked, "Benjamin, where is that new backpack I bought for you?"

"A big bear tore it off my back and ripped it to shreds while I was squeezing between two rocks."

When his mother heard that, she passed right out again. "Medic," somebody yelled.

Scott ran to his parents. They hugged him so tightly he thought his bones would break.

"We were so worried about you," his mother cried.

"Worried and proud at the same time," his father added.

"And we prayed for you a lot," his mother continued with tears in her eyes as her voice cracked. "Your dad even joined one of the search teams."

"You did?"

"Yes, and you know what?"

Scott shook his head.

"My team was the one that found a path marked with strings tied to bushes and direction arrows made from sticks."

"We did that."

"I know, but it was confusing at first because it only took us around in a big circle."

"Us, too," Scott laughed.

His dad continued, "Right then, I sat down on a rock and asked God that if my team wasn't the one to find you, that some other team would. That's when God put the idea in my mind of the lost sheep. My lamb was lost, and I would do anything to find you."

"Dad, that's the same story that kept us going. We figured our guides probably started looking right away, but I knew God would take care of us. He had to be. Just look at everything that's happened."

"Well it's good to have you back safe. I don't know what I would have done if you weren't found."

"Thanks, Dad. Okay if I go see the guys for a minute?"

"Sure."

Scott walked over to where Al and Benji were standing with their parents. The families were about to head to their cars when, from behind them, they heard someone holler, "Heeeeey!"

The boys turned around just as Brian grabbed all three and

tackled them to the ground. It looked like a rugby match had broken out as the four of them laughed, cried, and wrestled on the ground. Brian finally came up for air.

"I'm so glad you're okay. We sent out search parties for you right away, but in all that fog it was impossible to find you."

"That was our fault," Scott admitted.

"Well, I prayed for you guys. And I want to thank you for something, too."

"Thank us?" Scott asked. "We thought you'd be in a lot of trouble over us."

"I do have some explaining to do, that's true, but what you guys did up there may have saved a lot of people's lives. You protected my family, too. So, thank you."

Scott and Brian swapped email addresses so they could keep in touch. They also agreed to share any information and ideas about environmental questions in the future. Then he gave each of the guys a big hug before they drove away.

The colonel was right. For the first few days after they returned home, there was a twenty-four-hour, non-stop, news storm about their story. Scott ran the VCR at his house to record the news around the clock for the next several days just so he could relive the experience over, and over, and over again. Scott's father had to remind him not to get a big head from all the attention. Then the boys gathered at Scott's house for a pizza party and to watch more of the coverage on TV.

"We're famous!" Scott reminded his father.

"Well, believe it or not, it'll all pass. And when it does, things will have to get back to normal."

"Shhh," the boys said all at once. Their story came on again and a news anchorman began his report.

"An update now on those boys lost in the Rocky Mountains. A government source has revealed that documents seized in the mountain cabin raid yielded a sinister plot aimed at hurting as many people in crowded areas as possible. Additional arrests have been made in a number of undisclosed, foreign locations."

Benji watched intently, then in his usual worried style said, "That could have been bad . . . couldn't it?"

Al and Scott looked at each other and groaned,

"Benji!"

- The End -

Distress signs used for search amd rescue teams

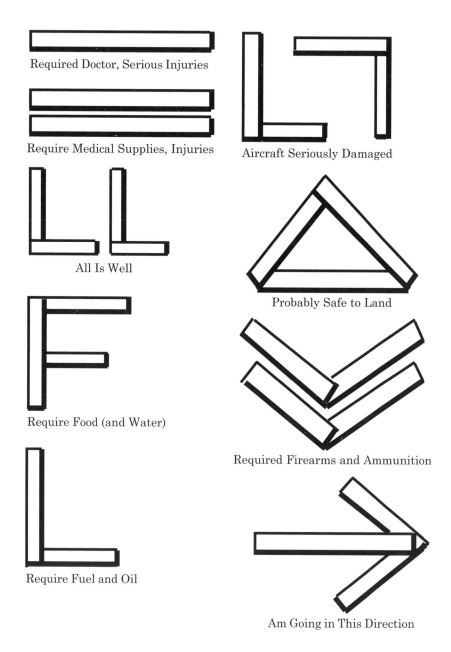

Required Doctor, Serious Injuries

Require Medical Supplies, Injuries

Aircraft Seriously Damaged

All Is Well

Probably Safe to Land

Require Food (and Water)

Required Firearms and Ammunition

Require Fuel and Oil

Am Going in This Direction

Other Max Elliot Anderson Books in the Tweener Adventure Series from Baker Trittin Press

NEWSPAPER CAPER - Tom Stevens was a super salesman. He and his friends delivered newspapers early every morning. Along their route, the boys often saw some pretty strange things. Then one day they actually became the story in their newspapers. Their adventures lead them to attack dogs, car thieves, and a frightening chop shop they uncover. This story reminds us of how important friendship is.

TERROR AT WOLF LAKE - Eddy Thompson was known for one thing and one thing only. Eddy was a cheater. He cheated on anything, anytime, anywhere, until something happened up at Wolf Lake. It wasn't the brutal cold. It wasn't when he fell through the ice. It wasn't even when two scary men arrived at their remote cabin. What happened would change Eddy's life . . . forever.

NORTH WOODS POACHERS - The Washburn families have been coming to the same cabins, on the same lake, catching the same fish, for about as long as Andy can remember. He is sick of it. This summer would be different. In the end, Andy learns the concepts family tradition and that God loves justice and hates injustice. Naturally, no one will ever forget Big Wally.

Other Books in the
Tweener Press Adventure Series
to be released in 2004:

BIG-RIG RUSTLERS

SECRET OF ABBOTT'S CAVE

LOST ISLAND SMUGGLERS

RECKLESS RUNAWAY

MAX ELLIOT ANDERSON

Max Elliot Anderson is a reluctant reader even though he grew up surrounded by books. In fact, his father has written more than 70 books. In spite of his attitude toward reading, he went on to graduate from college with a degree in psychology.

In an effort to determine why he didn't like to read, he discovered that for him the style of most children's books ". . . was boring, the dialog sometimes sparse, or when it was used, it seemed to adult." He set out to write books he would like to read . . . concise books with action, suspense, and humor. His adventure series ". . . is not where all these fantastic things that couldn't possibly happen to any *one* of us, happens to the same kids, in the same town, over and over again. Each book in the series has completely different characters, settings, and adventures."

Mr. Anderson is a Vietnam era veteran of the U.S. Army. Professionally, he has been involved in some of the most successful Christian films for children. His video productions earned many national awards including 3 Telly Awards (the equivalent of an Oscar). He was involved in a PBS television production that received an Emmy nomination and the double album won a Grammy.

He is 56 years old, married with two adult children. He can be reached at: PO Box 4126, Rockford, IL 61110
       Email Mander8813@aol.com

Order Information

If your favorite bookstore does not have *The Tweener Press Adventure Series* in stock, you can order them directly from the publisher for $10.95 plus $3.50 for shipping and handling per book (*Newspaper Carper* is $9.95 ea.). If five or more copies are ordered, send only $2.00 shipping and handling per book. Indiana residents add 6% sales tax.

Please send ____ copies of _____ @ $10.95 ea. _____

Please send ____ copies of _____ @ $10.95 ea. _____

Please send ____ copies of _____ @ $10.95 ea. _____

Indiana redidents please add 6% sales tax ($.66 per book)   _____

Shipping and handling @ $3.50 per book   _____

      ($2.00 per book for five or more)

                            TOTAL _____

PLEASE PRINT

      Name _____

      Address _____

      City _____ State _____ Zip _____

      Phone _____ email _____

      Credit Card # _____ Exp _____

      Name on Card _____

      Signature _____

Mail order blank with check or money order payable to Baker Trittin Press
Baker Trittin Press, P.O. Box 277, Winona Lake, IN 46590